MAIN CHICK VS SIDE BITCH

The Complete Series

SOLAE DEHVINE

Copyright © 2016 by Solae Dehvine

All rights reserved.

No part of this book may be reproduced in any form or by any electronic or mechanical means, including information storage and retrieval systems, without written permission from the author, except for the use of brief quotations in a book review.

To God for the Gift
To my Mother for the Foundation
To my Husband for the Belief
and To YOU for reading
I don't take any of this for granted
Thank you all for the blessings

Part I

1

DeWayne

My Daddy told me that back in the day he had more hoes than Macy's had clothes. Just think for a second about all the racks of clothes in Macy's and then imagine my Dad, the old mack with a slicked back ponytail strolling around with bitches on each arm.

But all the while he kept my Momma first and treated her like a queen and me like his prince in training, telling me everything I needed to know about a woman and her mentality.

I guess that's where I got this shit from because good pussy was always my weakness. Like a crack head fiend for the next hit I was always looking for a pair of thighs and fat ass to slide my dick between. That thinking always got me in trouble and while I know I have a problem, I'm still powerless to stop it. They say the first step is admitting your issues so yes, I admit it I'm addicted to pussy and fine bitches and I can't stop.

That addiction now had me in the back of my barber shop trying to calm my girl down. Kiara was a lawyer, fierce, a good cook, freak in the bed, and a banging body with a mouth piece that drove my dick crazy but she still wasn't enough. It wasn't about her, it was me and I could admit that so I promised her I would never leave her alone, but at the same time the dog needed to roam.

All of that brought me to now, going through our weekly routine of bullshit that always went the same way.

First Kiara, my girl, my fiancé, my love of my life gets a hint that I'm cheating. Today she jumped from her BMW, coming into the shop dressed in her a black suit straight from work, storming in, cursing in front of my customers. I haven't been home in a day or two and I told her I was chilling at my mom's which was the truth. But of course I wasn't alone and I guess she found out the truth.

Instead of having our argument in the middle of the shop for everyone to see, I brought her towards the back of the shop into a supply room where she could tell and curse all the fuck she wanted.

Her story was the same, yet again another bitch has come to my girl trying to fuck my shit up but they all knew I was never leaving her, I made that shit clear but it never stopped them from trying. What can I say, the bitches loved me but it was too bad I didn't love them. They may get to fuck me from time to time but my heart belongs to Kiara.

"Did you hear me, I said who is this bitch." I closed to the supply room door behind us shielding the rest of the shop from our business.

Kiara was so fucking mad, pushing the phone in my face but that shit only turned me on more so I played the game.

"I told you I don't know Keke." Kiara looked at me sideways as if she knew I was lying but she had no real proof, and with my lip poked out and a fresh hair cut I could persuade her of anything. She didn't know that under my barber apron and inside my jeans, my dick was pulsing wanting to fuck that pouty mean look right off her face. I looked her dead in her eyes a stare down that I had no intention of turning away from.

"Boo, straight up. I'm doing things the right way now. Look at the ring on your finger." I pointed to the two carat diamond that I just put on her left hand a month before, reminding her of what I said.

"So, why the fuck is she messaging me on IG claiming that she knows you?" Now that part was really a mystery. I told every bitch that I fucked with to keep their mouth closed and stay away from Kiara.

It wasn't no mystery that me and Keke were together and it seemed like the longer we stayed together the more hoes wanted to fuck with me but I played the shit off.

"Girl, who wouldn't want to fuck with me? Shit, everybody knows me." I rubbed my fade smiling at her but it was true. Every bitch in the city wanted a piece of this chocolate thunder and I couldn't blame them. From the brown eyes, mocha skin, and chiseled arms, it was no way to keep these chicks off me. But no matter how many of them I fucked with, Kiara was always my ace, the last card in my deck, and the one who always picked me up when I was down. I pulled her close as she thought about what I said.

"But she said she was riding in your car. Described the car and everything in it." Kissing her neck and I heard a small moan. I knew every spot on this woman's body and with my hands wrapped around her curves I knew I only had to touch a few other places and she would let this shit go.

"Keke come on now. Everybody knows what car I drive. We like celebrities around this bitch." I pushed the phone down as she let me kiss her on the mouth. Our tongues smashing together like she hadn't seen me in years instead of days.

"No no...you always run this bullshit and I back down. Explain..." but I silenced her with my tongue between her lips and pulled her into me. My dick poking out from my jeans hitting her right near her pussy. She couldn't resist knowing that only a few pieces of clothing separated her from the stick she had been addicted to for the last five years. Now it was my turn to run the show but she pushed me with tears falling down her cheeks.

"You're always doing this shit, trying to turn it around on me." Bringing her hand up, she barely missed smacking me in the face.

"Damn, you gonna hit me." Pinning her back against the wall, I kissed her harder this time. Her leg stretching up and wrapping around my hips as I held both of her hands over her head.

I knew what she wanted, Keke acted big and bad but it wasn't shit that this dick couldn't handle.

"Look here prosecutor. I need you to calm all that down." She bit at my lip as I tried to talk, forcing me to push all of my weight on her, I knew she felt my dick for sure now.

"How you gonna make me calm down?" She ran her leg up and down mine and that confirmed it, she came in here barking like the big bad wolf but she was going to leave walking crooked.

Letting her hands go I picked her up, her legs now wrapped around my waist as I pinned her to the wall. Pulling my dick out with my jeans dropping to the floor, it only took seconds for me to slide her panties to the side and enter her ocean.

She gasped as I entered her, my flesh sliding into her juices. Keke was the only girl I hit raw, all the other bitches got the latex dick but my baby got the real deal. I pumped inside her, spreading her open with every thrust of my dick as she moaned.

"Damn boy…" She moaned louder and louder, I was sure the entire shop could hear her by now and I knew she did that shit on purpose so I played along.

"Who's pussy is this?" I asked her, letting her down and pushing her over the towel table. Hand towels flew to the floor as Keke gripped the sides of the table.

I slapped her fat round ass with it turned up to me and her skirt around her waist.

"I said…who's pussy is this." Diving inside her she screamed loud, her voice filling the room. I pushed a towel in her mouth fucking her so hard that my hips clapped against her ass.

I heard her screaming my name through the towel and that's what I liked to hear.

"Don't…bring…yo…ass…back…up…here…to…my…shop…acting.. HEAR ME." I pounded harder as she moaned through the towel.

Keke was my bitch. I trained her, my dick knew every curve of her pussy like a tunnel I created. She was mine and she wasn't going anywhere. Yeah I had other bitches but she was my main chick and everyone knew that. And this was the way this shit was going to stay.

2

Ariane

I hustled like a man but I was all woman and even though I've been on my feet all day braiding hair, I told DeWayne that I would be moving into my booth tonight. At nine o'clock at night with it being dark outside I wanted to be at home under the sheets, but I was walking into Cutting Edge Barbershop and Salon.

Men were standing around looking me up and down as I walked through the door but I didn't care, this place was going to be my big start.

I saw this place as my rebirth after being locked down for so long. This place meant no more prison, orange jumpsuits and trifling bitches. I was free now and everyday since my feet touched the free soil I have been hustling like a bitch with ten kids with no baby daddy in sight.

I have to get it on my own because ain't nobody trying to help a grown woman, especially a grown woman with felonies.

Coming in the shop, everybody was quiet, the TV was turned down and the few barbers that were cutting were quieter than mice.

"Hey everybody." But my hi's were only returned with shushes. This was way different than the salon I visited a week ago but I didn't say shit. I wasn't here to make friends so I unpacked at the station that DeWayne said I could have when I heard it.

"Who's pussy is this?" It was clear but the voice still sounded far away. I turned around thinking it was someone's cell phone or maybe some porno that the guys were playing on the TV but turning around they were all smiling, silently giving each other fives.

One of the barbers pointed to the back room whispering. "D back there getting his chick together," he smiled but I was irritated. How was I supposed to bring women into a place like this? Where niggas sat around listening to the hoe ass owner have sex with chicks in the other room.

I rolled my eyes and kept working. If this wasn't the most popular salon in the city I wouldn't be here, especially if DeWayne wasn't offering to give me a whole month of free booth rent.

Before this I was working out of my house, trying to make things pop there and it worked until shit got way too big for me to be braiding hair out of my kitchen.

DeWayne hit me up online and the rest was history but now, looking around at these thirsty ass bums I was rethinking my choice, this wasn't just a barbershop and salon. In the back there was a full-fledged clothing store that all the dope boys shopped at. And dope boys always had girlfriends and that was where my money was about to come in.

I needed this place, and it was the missing ingredient to pulling my hustle up, I just had to survive stupid shit like this.

I pretended not to hear what sounded like ass clapping,

eventually my mind jumped to my little girl. Wondering what she was doing and if she missed me.

I was in prison for five years, the first five years of my daughters life and the longest five years of mine. Through that time I thought of her everyday, I cried so hard that it made me sick sometimes.

I was doing this for her, looking my baby in the eyes through the Plexiglas on them visits killed me. So now I didn't care if I had to braid one hundred heads a week, listen to bitches fuck all day, and deal with these thirst bucket ass niggas all day if it meant I could get my little girl back.

A door slammed snapping me out of my trance.

Looking up I saw a woman in a business suit walking from the back with her head held high but a noticeable dip in her step.

I guess that's who he was fucking. I could already tell by the way the guys looked at her or better yet tried NOT to look her way.

She was gone from the shop, disappearing into the parking lot.

I saw a car pull out, brake lights and then nothing, she left.

A few minutes later, DeWayne emerged with the peanut gallery laughing and clapping. This was the shit I would have to deal with.

"You was killing her ass back there dawg." I wanted to laugh at these clown ass niggas. They all acted like they haven't had any pussy in years. Meanwhile I hadn't fucked a man in five years, since I got locked up. My pussy was tighter than cheerio, but sex was the last thing on my mind.

"Y'all need to chill man."

"Hey shorty. What up?" he was talking to me. I had

been warned about DeWayne, his reputation with women wasn't that great but I wasn't worried about his ass.

I wasn't one of these dumb ass bitches that wanted to get their son a free haircut so they would fuck DeWayne or give him head so their son could have a good fade.

I'm a businesswoman, so if DeWayne wasn't talking about money and business then we had nothing to talk about.

"Hey DeWayne, I'm just getting situated for in the morning. You said that you were going to give me keys so I could get started early."

"Aww fuck..." he shook his head. "I forgot shorty...I'll just come up here and meet you."

"Ummm, my first appointment is at 6 o'clock in the morning." This was the shit I was talking about but I kept it cool.

"I'm here every morning at six. I got my wholesalers that come in at that time."

"Wholesalers?" I asked because anything that sounded like money I needed to know about but we were cut off.

"Yo DeWayne, I knocked off all them hats homie. I need some more." A man handed DeWayne so much money that my eyes almost popped out of my head.

"Cool man. Let's go back to the store. I got you." He began to walk away but he turned around, those brown eyes sparkling.

"I'll holla at you in the morning shorty. I'll be here at six." I nodded hoping he was telling the truth but the way this man moved let me know he was all about business.

My phone ringing stole my thoughts.

My lawyers name across my phone had me making my way outside before I answered.

"Hello." Mr. Fabri calling me this late only meant bad news.

"Ariane. Mr Fabri here. Is this a bad time?"

"No sir, go right ahead." Anytime he called, I dropped everything to hear what he had to say.

"Sorry to call so late but I got a hearing scheduled today for your case." The case he spoke of was my custody case with my daughter's father. He was fighting every bit of the way to have my rights to my child taken away. I carried her for nine months and just because I got locked up he had to step up and be a father.

"Okay, when is it?"

"Three week's from today." I felt like throwing up.

"Three weeks?" I at least thought we would get a couple of months. That would give me enough time to get my money together.

"Yes, we need to get this done quickly so I need a few things from you." I breathed deep hearing that. There was always something that I needed to do but I opened my ears, breathing deep and waited for Mr. Fabri to drop some knowledge on me.

"You need to have a place, gainful employment, a vehicle is a plus, and make sure that you pay me the next few payments on time so there is no lapse in my service to you." He couldn't forget about himself or the five thousand he wanted to take the case.

"Sure sir, I will make sure I do that." I owned him a thousand dollars in a few days and I was almost there but it was going to take some grinding to get my daughter back.

"Good. I'll talk to you soon, maybe a week before the hearing so we can get our ducks in a row." If nothing else the man was thorough.

We hung up with an understanding. I wanted my daughter back and the only person that could help me was my lawyer and he wanted five stacks.

Main Chick vs Side Bitch

I looked at Faded Focus and that only left one thing for me to do. And that was grind.

3

Ariane

After talking to Mr. Fabri last night, I didn't sleep that well. Bitches invaded my thoughts taking me back to my days in prison. Not the pleasant days where my time was a breeze but those days that were so hard on me that I thought I was going to die. Those nights where I cried myself to sleep with a picture of my daughter clutched in my hands. Those nights when I cried so silently that I don't think God could even hear me.

Now that I was out, in my own place with my own furniture and a lock on the door I still didn't feel safe.

I stayed up most of the night looking at braiding designs, watching YouTube videos for ideas for my clients and then I put up more ads to get even more customers. I'm like a fucking gorilla out here, I needed this money or everything in my life was going to crumble.

Getting to the shop, what I saw made me almost afraid to get out of the car.

There were cars everywhere with white people jumping out and walking up to the shop. At first I saw white people, early in the morning and I thought about when I got arrested. I thought about the feds coming and snatching me out of my bed and taking me away for some shit I did that I didn't understand.

I shook that shit off as I walked into the shop. Music was blasting and DeWayne was already there talking to people like it was six at night and not six in the morning.

Of course on my way in I saw a text from my client saying she wasn't coming. That was the story of my life. But I decided I would stay up, go into the shop and figure out how to get my schedule full by the end of the day.

"What up shorty?" DeWayne screamed from the back. I guessed that was my new name or maybe he didn't even remember my name. I guess remembering names was reserved for the bitches he was fucking.

"Hey wassup."

"Your key is on your station." He was right, he told the truth as I walked over a gold key was laying right on the top of my station.

"Hey Ariane, I want you to meet Lisa. She had a cancellation on her hair appointment and I told her you are the baddest in the land. Here I was not even taking my coat off and DeWayne was already introducing people to me.

"Hi, nice to meet you."

"Girl, DeWayne showed me your work. You are fire…how much do you charge and when can you fit me in." I felt like I was on the moon.

"Well it depends on what you want done but I can do it right now. I had a cancellation." The woman's eyes got big as boulders.

"Let me go get my hair. I gotta run home and I'll be right back. I don't care how much you charge, I'm doing it," she laughed and ran out promising to come back.

"Damn D. Thanks I really appreciate that." I went

over to his station still in shock at what just happened. Usually women had a million questions for me trying to figure out who I am and what they wanted but that chick was ready to go.

"You treat Lisa right and she will be in your chair every week. She comes in here to buy clothes and shit for her boutique and she has more money than you can imagine." I felt like I was walking on air. God told me that I would be getting a blessing by coming here.

"I really appreciate it. My client didn't show up and…"

"Rule number 1 in this business, when doing what you are doing. You need to get deposits. Make them hoes keep their appointments because every missed appointment is money you ain't making…you dig?" He was putting me up on game and I listened to every word. I nodded as he kept talking. Telling me about how he got started in the industry and was charging five dollars for haircuts just to get people in the door.

"Now these niggas gotta pay at least $75 to sit in my chair." I soaked up everything he told me, he reminded me so much of Paul, my baby daddy when we first met. Paul gave me the game back then showing that he cared for me and wanted to look out for a young chick like me. Back then it wasn't braiding or cutting hair, the game was cocaine and heroine but even though the game changed the love was still the same.

"You feel me though, you just gotta push this shit." I felt him alright, I knew exactly what was going on. From the way he was looking at me and every few words he would put his hands on my shoulder.

"I know what you been through shorty. You bring in some money to this shop and this shop will give money to you, aight?"

"Yeah, I get it D. Thank you." I put my hand on his

Main Chick vs Side Bitch

shoulder, looking into his eyes as he looked into mine. What the fuck happened between yesterday and today that made this man look so damn fine to me.

The door opened and I turned my head only to see some chick at the door with her arms crossed and a frown on her face. D quickly brushed me off and looking a little closer I recognized her as the chick from yesterday.

"Really...this is what you needed to come into the shop early for?" The bitch was damn near screaming.

"Hey...calm all that down man..."

"Who is this bitch?" I felt me face get hot as the bitch walked closer with her heels clanking on the shop floor. D looked back and forth from her to me not saying anything so I had to defend myself.

"First of all. I'm not a bitch, my name is Ariane." I put out my hand to shake hers and let the bitch know there was no me trying to brush on her man but she looked at my hand like I had shit on my fingers.

"Like I said DeWayne...who is this bitch in my shop?" I was about to say something but Tori, one of the other stylists grabbed me and pulled me back.

"Chill girl...that's Ms. Boss Bitch. That's what I call her." She was whispering as this chick got all in DeWayne's face.

"She was about to be Ms. Get her ass whooped. Who the fuck is she?" We talked while the chick and DeWayne argued. I felt like we were on a talk show. It was way too early for this shit and what bitch comes to a man's job and argues with him while he works?

"Girl, that is Kiara "Keke" Lawrence. The co-owner of the shop, DeWayne's main chick, and a big time lawyer." Tori was giving me the low down on this bitch. "She always popping in here going off on DeWayne. Sometimes he takes her in the back, fucks the shit out of

17

her and she's cool." Tori laughed and I figured it out, that's what was going on last night but today it was a different tune.

I sat back in the salon chair peeping the whole scene, the bitch was insecure and it showed. Yeah, she dressed nice in her business suit, yesterday I remembered her having on a black skirt but today it was slacks and a blazer to match. Her heels were expensive, some designer that I couldn't think of and her hair was laid in some up do with curls and not to mention the BMW keys that were dangling from her hand. She was definitely paid, and she was cute, but DeWayne needed someone strong that wouldn't be on his back everyday.

He was a hustler, I could tell and the only thing that hustlers appreciated was money, not some nagging bitch always on his back.

"You see you all in here with this bitch but you didn't even answer me back about the meeting tonight." DeWayne rolled his eyes as I cracked my knuckles. Boss bitch and part owner of the salon or not, I wasn't about to be too many more bitches from this stuck up insecure hoe.

I beat bitches down in prison that were ten times bigger and badder than her, and here there were no guards to stop me.

"What did I tell you about cursing and causing a scene man." DeWayne got in her face, finally checking the bitch like he should have when she came through the door. "I gotta go see about my kids tonight. You do remember that I do have other responsibilities besides you Keke." She pouted, her lip poking out like a toddler.

"But you promised, it's a meeting with the partners and I need you there." But DeWayne shook his head.

"Junior has a basketball game tonight and I promised I

would be there and take him and his sister to dinner. I can't back out…"

"Well, fine then. See if I keep putting money into this shop and paying your bills and shit…" He grabbed her arm, pulling her out the door before she could say anything else. Tori laughed as soon as the door closed leaving us alone in the shop.

"Honey…that bitch is a trip. I don't know how she stays with DeWayne's old dog ass anyway." Tori talked while she cleaned up her station.

"What you mean?"

"Girl, DeWayne is the biggest hoe in town. He has babies all over and Keke's ass is stupid enough to stay with him. She gives that nigga money and everything." Tori shook her head but I was too busy watching them argue outside the window. I wished I could hear what they were saying.

"But I thought DeWayne got his own money." Tori laughed.

"Don't get me wrong. D is a hustler and all but Keke is a big time lawyer, that bitch makes well into the six figures." I nodded my head thinking of a master plan as I watched the scene outside. Keke slapped D and walked to her car, leaving him in front of the shop holding his face and shouting.

"Ohh wee…I guess he didn't give in to what she wanted." Tori said just what I was thinking. "But don't get all bent out of shape. She gets like that with people when she sees somebody pushing up on D." I had to stop her.

"I wasn't pushing up…"

"Honey please…I saw the way he looks at your ass. How he was with you the first day you interviewed to come in the shop. Ole girl sees it too and she is threatened." I laughed that shit off as D came back in the shop with a frown deep on his face.

"I'm sorry y'all had to experience that. I'm gonna make sure shit like that doesn't happen anymore. And I'm sorry she disrespected you Ariane." He came over to me, shaking my hand but that look in his eye said way more. Maybe Tori was right about what she saw.

"No worries D. Lets get this money. I think I got some people that might want some of your merchandise back in the store." His eyes lit up.

"Word...call em up. I'll give you a commission on everything they buy. Straight up." He was excited again, his eyes dancing like nothing ever happened and that solidified it for me. This man was a hustler and he needed a real bitch that was going to bring him money, make him feel powerful, and not stress him out.

"That's wassup. I'll get them right over here. We can all eat." I told him and winked. He smiled at that and a plan jumped into my head.

I knew it from that moment on that Ms. Kiara had a right to feel threatened because I was about to steal her man. And most of all, there was no way she was going to stop me.

4

Kiara

I was established with a career, a 790 credit score, no children, and a banging body that supermodels would beg for. All of these things going for me I should be dating a stockbroker or a doctor but instead I fell in love with DeWayne Sherief Coleman five years ago. Since then, I haven't been able to shake him.

When I try to leave, he keeps pestering me, showing up at my office, my home, and even calling my mother. It was like a trap and like an idiot I let him stay and roll back into my life.

Maybe it was the dick or that he sucked my pussy so good that he made me bust all over his face, but whatever the reason I couldn't leave DeWayne alone.

Here I was, an educated woman that sat in courtrooms deciding million dollar cases all day and I was still chasing hood rats away from my man and dealing with his issues. From the kids, to the hoes and the lies, I still allowed him to stay around and of course no one could understand why.

To be honest, I didn't know myself, I guess it is just love

or maybe stupidity but DeWayne had me wrapped around his finger.

My day started out by waking up to a cold bed, again DeWayne said he was coming home but that was yet another lie. And then I went to the shop to confront him about it only to find him hugged up with some braider bitch.

I was pissed, ready to throw this ring back in his face but instead I slapped his ass and went to work. I worked for one of the most prestigious law firms in the city Puzder, Thomas, and Brown where I was trying my damnedest to make junior partner.

If I wasn't at work, I was at home thinking and reading up for work. This job outside of DeWayne was my life and it took me by surprised that he had a lame excuse for why he couldn't come with me tonight to see about our future.

The shop, DeWayne's car, and most of his clothes were financed by me and my job. I'm the type of person to put the money where her mouth is and if I believe in you I will put everything I have behind my man to bring him up to my standards.

When I met DeWayne he was struggling in barber school and living in his mother's basement. He didn't even own a suit let alone a sports jacket and a pair of loafers. Now the man had a thriving business thanks to me, a closet full of clothes, a passport, an investment portfolio, but what he lacked was focused.

It was my fault, I showed him too much too quickly and now he didn't know how to keep his dick out of these skeezers and his mind on our empire.

I thought about all of that now as I drove across town, racing to the business meeting with one of the partners that DeWayne was supposed to be at with me but instead I was calling him on the phone.

After what I just found out I wished I could go to him and slap him in his face a second time but I was running late.

Over the hands-free system in my BMW I called the man that was supposed to be my fiancé and ask him a question about our credit card bill.

"Hello?" He answered like he was still upset but it was me that had the right to be mad.

"What did you buy on our credit card for eight thousand dollars?" I got right to the point. Driving with one hand, holding the bill with the other and trying not to smash into cars as I sped down the highway.

"Eight thousand…" He tried playing dumb. "I didn't buy shit for eight thousand dollars?" He and I were the only two people in the world with cards for this account. It was bad when I had to play lawyer with my own fucking fiancé.

"DeWayne Coleman. What did you purchase from Zephyr jewelry store for eight thousand dollars?" The phone was silent for a moment.

"Oh…from Zephyr. That's the ring, your engagement ring." I looked down at my left hand, the ring that shined bright that I was so excited to get, now felt like fire on my finger.

"So you mean to tell me I am paying for my own engagement ring?" I felt like jumping through the phone and killing him.

"Babe c'mon now. You know I'm gonna give the money back. But they had the ring and I didn't want to let it go."

"What the fuck do you mean pay me back DeWayne. This is American Express, I have to pay this bill off every month." He sounded like such a fucking idiot and I had to watch my credit meticulously around him.

"Awww well shit. I thought it was one of those one year no interest joints. I figured I could pay that off in a year." He laughed but shit wasn't funny to me. If I knew I was buying my own engagement ring I would have proposed to myself, it would have been cheaper that way.

"DeWayne, you are such a fuck up when it comes to money." I merged off the highway tossing the credit card bill in the back seat of the car. It disgusted me to even look at it right now knowing that I would have to pay a huge eight thousand dollar bill that I wasn't anticipating. I had the money but DeWayne spent so much on the shop as if I was made of money.

"Aww baby don't be like that," he laughed a bit, like this was eight dollars and not eight thousand. "You know we make way more than that."

"Correction...I make way more than that. What you pull in from the shop goes on you, your child support, and whatever bitch you are fucking for the night." He stopped laughing when I said that and everything I was telling him was the truth. I would have cried if I had time but up ahead was the Grand Laury hotel, my destination for tonight's dinner.

"I told you I don't want or need your money."

"But you never refuse it."

"Whatever man. Is that all you wanted?" Now he wanted to get off the phone when I was speaking the truth.

"Are you one hundred percent not joining me for dinner with Mr. Puzder?" I had to make sure as I pulled into the valet line in the front of the hotel.

"I told you, man. I got the fucking game tonight I can't do it…."

"Fine DeWayne, tell ya baby momma I said hi." I hung up on his ass just in time as the valet attendant, clad in a red jacket and black slacks, came to open my door.

"Thank you." I passed him a couple of dollars and headed inside in search of my boss Mr. Chris Puzder. He was a senior partner and one of the people that would be voting in a couple of days on whether I would be partner or not.

Zipping into the hotel lobby, I calmed down, breathing deep and following the signs for the Met restaurant that was in the far corner of the hotel.

Seeing Mr. Puzder I smiled and acted as if nothing was wrong, putting all of my issues and problems with DeWayne aside, this was business and to nail my goals I had to be on top of my game for this meeting.

"Mr. Puzder. Sorry I'm late." He stood and I shook his hand and took my seat."

"No problem, just nursing a vodka tonic." He smiled his chiseled white teeth against his brown skin. I felt proud to be sitting across from the man that had been through so many obstacles to become senior partner, as a black man in any law firm was a definite miracle.

But now his name was first in the line of partners for the firm and when this man said he wants to sit down and talk, me as an up and coming candidate for partner, I can do nothing but clear my schedule.

"Would you like something to drink Miss?" the waiter was at the table within seconds.

"I will have a glass of Riesling please." I smiled, unbuttoning my blazer and taking a full breath.

"How is the Smithston case coming along?" he got right down to business asking me about one of the biggest case I was overseeing.

"It's going great. The jury is in deliberation and we are hoping to hear a decision tomorrow."

"Good good. I know you have it in the bag. That will be a huge settlement to add to the firm's record." Everything was about winning percentages and how many cases have you tried and how many have you won. For me my win column far exceeded my loses and that was why I had this opportunity.

"Yes sir, it will. And as soon as I make partner I would love to continue to win even bigger cases." I had my eyes on this prize from way back in law school when I completed an internship with the company. Mr. Puzder took an eye to me then, taking me under his wing and giving me different material to read and absorb. Most of that was why I was such a great attorney today.

The waiter returned with my glass of wine and I sipped it, paying attention to Mr. Puzder's every word.

"Well, the partnership voting is the reason I called you here." My heart beat rapidly in my chest as he spoke. "You see there are quite a few qualified attorney's up this year for vote but the board definitely has its eye on you." I was glad to hear that. I had worked my ass off and did all the right things to be at this moment.

"Thank you sir. I appreciate you being so candid with me." He didn't have to tell me any of this so I was grateful. I felt like two black people sticking together in the firm was exactly what was needed so we could pull more young attorneys up.

"Well I'm glad you respect me being candid." He guzzled down the rest of his drink looking directly in my eyes.

"You see, I am willing to vote for you and persuade a few of the other members as well. But I would need you to do something for me." I smiled at that. I was willing to help Mr. Puzder out in any way I could. A few times I took on extra cases or handled a few briefs for his personal clients for free just to be helpful.

"Sure sir, anything I can do to help." He smiled at that

placing his glass down he reached into his jacket pocket and pulled out a card of some sort and slide it across the table.

Upon further examination, I saw it wasn't just a card but a key...a room key.

"That is for my suite. Room 1122. It's the presidential," he bragged on his room selection but I wasn't understanding where this was going.

"What's in your room sir?" He smiled, signaling for the waiter to bring the check.

"Well you see Ms. Lawrence, this industry is all about nepotism. It's who you know and who is willing to help you out." I felt like my heart was in my shoes now as I glanced back and forth from him to the room key. "There are quite a few people, as I told you, that would love to be partner, but we only have space for two." I swallowed as he scratched his face with his left hand, his wedding ring shining in my face.

"But I am the most qualified, my win percentage…"

"Damn your win percentage sweetie. I need more than a fucking win percentage to place a vote for you." He pushed the key closer to my side of the table. "You can come up to my suite and fully persuade me or I can go along with one of the other candidates that is willing. No harm, no foul," he shrugged it off as the waiter brought the check.

"And if I don't…"

"Well, there is always next year." I felt my head start to pound with a headache. Mr. Puzder was attractive for an older man, his salt and pepper goatee was striking but I never considered sex with him. I always wanted to be taken seriously in this industry and not as some whore lying on her back to get paid.

"Next year there will be twice as many candidates but

with only one seat." Every other year the firm alternated between two seats for partner and then back to one. This year was my best chance to get in.

"Well my dear, that is true, so it seems you have a decision to make." He licked his lips at me, his eyes dipping down my blouse. I felt so dirty, like a pig wallowing in mud and shit as he kept eye contact with me. He pulled out a stack of money from his other breast pocket and peeled off dollars and threw them on top of the bill without even bothering to look at it.

"It's your choice dear. Do what you think is best. No hard feelings." With that the man that I thought was my mentor stood up, buttoned his suit jacket, and strolled out of the restaurant leaving me at the table thinking hard about what the hell to do.

I grabbed my phone when I couldn't see him anymore, dialing DeWayne but five rings later the phone went to voicemail.

I needed to hear my man's voice, have him tell me it would be alright but instead I was sent to voicemail like some discarded hoe.

You're on your own. My mind told me and it was the truth, I had always been on my own. I swallowed down the Riesling in seconds and as the waiter returned to grab the bill I made a request.

"Get me a vodka double on the rocks and put it on room 1122." He nodded and was gone in a flash. If I was going to do this I needed as much liquor in my system as possible, because the way I saw it. I had two choices, be a bum attorney or be a wealthy partner with one night of indiscretion that I would never have to think about again.

The choice was simple, as the waiter came back with my vodka double I chugged it like I was back in college.

The burning of the liquid hitting the back of my chest and sizzling as it went down.

I was already horny, my pussy throbbing from being pissed at DeWayne in the car. Now all I had to do was imagine that Mr. Puzder was actually someone I wanted to fuck.

Standing up on wobbly legs I grabbed the hotel room key and made my way to the elevators. Inside, I swiped the room key and pressed the eleventh floor so I could go get this over with. I breathed deep, feeling the heat of the vodka coursing through my veins with every floor we climbed and my courage rising just like the elevator.

I had no mother, no father, no sisters or brothers to depend on. I worked my ass off through law school so I could live a life where I would never have to ask anyone for shit. Because in essence there was no one to ask.

Now stepping off the elevator and walking a few steps to get to room 1122, the only thing that was standing in my way of huge wealth was a door and an old man that wanted a small taste of me just to make a vote. That was nothing compared to the shit I had been through coming up and if this was what it took then so be it.

I was just about to slide the key into the door when my phone rang. I scrambled, grabbing my purse to silence it only to see DeWayne's name on the screen.

"Too late now baby." I whispered rejecting his call and turning my phone off. I had already made up my mind. I was going to make partner or die, and I wasn't dying anytime soon. Sliding the key into the door and twisting the nob I had settled this.

Kiara Lawrence was a winner and winners did what they had to by any means necessary.

5

DeWayne

So what, I bought Kiara's engagement ring with the platinum American Express, I needed to get her off my back from some shit that popped off last month and proposing was my only way to do it. Plus, my money needed to go towards other things, she doesn't know about every kid I got out here and all these bitches got they motherfucking hand out but today, my newest addition to Cutting Edge was showing out.

"Hey D. I want you to meet Delo. He wanted to buy the last of the hats." Ariane came back to the store in the back of the shop, but shit, it didn't feel like much of a store anymore. Since this morning she was bringing niggas in left and right. Dope boys that had cash to spend and they spent it all with me, buying out almost all of my inventory leaving the walls and the shelves practically bare.

I was so damn busy I ended up missing my son's basketball game.

I gave the dude in front of me some some dap as he looked over the last few hats I had laying on a display case.

"I'm gonna go finish up my client." She smiled and

winked at me as she walked away. This bitch had brought me more money in one day then anybody else in the shop.

As she walked off, I watched her ass swaying. Nothing made me want to fuck more than counting money and today, just from selling all of my merchandise all four of my pockets were full.

"Yo fam. I'll take all of these." The dude Delo grabbed all seven of the snapback hats I had left. He cashed me out and I put all of his purchases in a bag trying not to smile too hard.

"Here you go fam. I appreciate the support."

"No prob at all. Anything for Ariane she's a real down ass chick." I nodded as he talked.

"What you mean. Down like how?" I needed to know since I worked so close with her. She told me about a few of the things in her past but she didn't get specific.

"Man, she was facing twenty in the feds and she didn't say a word. We thought for sure that she would turn on us but she held it down. She beat a few charges and a couple stuck and then she walked down them five years like a champ." Damn, he was right. I didn't know one bitch that would go to jail and not squeal.

That was the main reason I got out of the dope game because I didn't want to go to jail. But for a chick to do a bid and not say shit was interesting.

"That's wassup fam. Thanks." I gave dude his stuff and he was gone into the night. As I came up front, Ariane was spraying oil over her client's hair and handing her a mirror.

"That looks good shorty, you got skills." She smiled as the client handed back the mirror and money.

"Here is a tip boo. Thanks for fitting me in." I smiled at that, we were all getting money today.

"Thanks Ms. Carol, be careful out there." Ariane

walked the woman to the door and watched her get into her car.

"Go ahead and lock the door. I'm done for the night." Looking at the time it was already pushing ten. I wasn't sure whether to go home and argue with Keke or just go over my moms and crash for the night.

"What a day." Ariane said as she swept hair up from the floor and she was more than right. Today was like some shit I had never seen before with people coming in to get cuts. New customers that I had never seen before and then with the clients for the clothes and apparel that Ariane brought in, I felt like a millionaire.

I pulled a stack out of my pocket and counted out two bills for her. She made me at least two stacks today so I could at least give her that.

"Here you go shorty."

"Damn...I appreciate that." She was sexy as fuck. The way she smiled and carried herself and old boy that was just in here confirmed it. She was a straight ride or die but I shook it off. I had to stay focused.

"Yo lets get out of here. I need to get home and deal with the wifey." I grabbed the broom from her.

"Cleaning crew is coming through tonight anyway, they will get all of this up."

"Damn, y'all got a cleaning crew. At every shop I went to everybody had to clean on certain nights." I laughed at that.

"After working hard all day who wants to clean up when we can include that in the booth rent and have cleaners come through every night." I wasn't running no bullshit ass establishment, this shop was going to be spotless and all of my people working in it were going to be happy.

"Well cool. Let me get my purse." I didn't hear shorty

complain, not once today, she was cool going with the flow of shit and working the entire time.

I cut off all the lights, turned on the alarm and we were out of the shop.

"You did good today. You keep bring in the customers like that and I'm gonna continue to kick you down a commission." I told her as I locked up the shop.

"Cool, I'm all about the money. Whatever it takes." I wasn't sure if I liked how she said that. There was something in her voice and the way the words just eased out of her mouth, I instantly thought of her sucking my dick.

I was fucking up, this always happened. I would get a good chick in the shop and somehow she would turn me on and I would end up fucking her. I shook my head walking to my car.

Those were old mistakes, young nigga shit but I was getting older and I couldn't keep doing the same things.

"Aight, good night." She got in her car waving and I got into mine. I was going to keep this shit with old girl strictly professional and that would be all.

I waited for her to start her car and leave the lot and taking some time to call Keke so we could start this arguing shit but her phone was still going to voicemail.

Earlier she called and I called her right back and she sent me to voicemail, true petty shit from Kiara but I probably had something to do with that.

When I met her she wasn't like this, she was cool and laid back and we used to fuck for days held up in her condo.

Now it was like all we did was fight but one thing my baby did was take care of money and she put me on in ways that women like her never would have taken the time to do.

A tap on my window shook me from my trance.

I rolled down my window for Ariane and she was almost in tears.

"My damn car won't start." I was no mechanic but I got out anyway trying to figure out what was wrong.

"Pop the hood." She jumped in the car and did as I said as I looked around at a bunch of shit I didn't know about.

She tried starting the car and she was right it wouldn't even turn over. I jiggled the battery, looked to see if any belts were snapped and when all of that looked okay I didn't have any ideas.

"How am I going to get to work in the morning?" I wanted to laugh at her.

"Girl, you made a lot of bread today. You can get this fixed, I'm sure it's simple. Hell I'll come get you for work tomorrow if I have to." Shit why did I say that. Me riding around the city in my caddy with her was like suicide. My black Escalade courtesy of Keke was for me only, if she caught me in there with another chick she would flip out for real.

"Really. Oh my God, thank you. You are just too nice to me." Only if she knew I wanted to be more than nice to her. I heard some sirens and it was getting late, no need in us sitting around looking at the car.

"Let me get you home. I'm tired." I was telling the truth I really was tired but watching her fat ass walk back to my car only made me want to think about smashing her but I made myself a promise. No more mixing ass with business, and I was gonna try my damnedest to stick to that shit.

6

Ariane

My car not starting was some divine intervention shit, that and the fact that I was out of gas and I already knew that. But D had no idea and that was the way I wanted to keep it. Now I needed to figure out a way to get him into my house.

We drove along not saying much as I thought about what I could do.

Originally I was going to wait, take time seducing him but my pussy was talking to me. Telling me that too much time had passed and I needed something long and strong and a vibrator wasn't going to cut it tonight.

I wasn't sure if this was too soon but only time would tell. If I couldn't get him in my house then maybe it wasn't meant to be but in the past, whatever I wanted, I got.

"It's that house right there, on the left."

"Cool." He threw the car in park. "You mind if I come in and use your bathroom. I need to wash some of this oil off my hands." Bingo, I felt like I won the lottery.

"Sure, that's the least I could do to show my appreciation." I touched his arm but he shook it off as we got out.

This was perfect and walking up to the house I felt like this was a way better way to make things happen than what I was thinking.

Letting him in, I pointed down the hall.

"It's down there and the first door on your left." Thankfully I wasn't no dirty bitch and my house was clean so there was nothing to be embarrassed about. When I heard the door close on the bathroom I knew I only had a few minutes.

I went for gold, taking my clothes off and putting on some music from my phone.

It felt like it took hours for me to get undressed but I sat on the couch, naked and ready for whatever was about to happen.

Hearing the water cut off, I breathed deep hoping he liked what he saw.

"Aight, I'm about to…" He came back into the living room at a loss with his mouth hanging open and that's when I knew I had him.

"What's going on shorty like…"

"Like what you mean. You ain't neva seen no pussy before." That shut him up, he just stared at me looking from me to the door so I made it easy, standing up and going to him when his damn phone started ringing. I knew before he looked that it was that bitch.

"Fuck her, I bet she can't suck your dick like I can." I pushed him up against the wall, kissing on his neck as he answered the phone.

"Helll…o" He didn't push me away so I kept going. Lowering down to my knees unbuckling his belt and letting his jeans fall to his knees.

I heard a woman's voice but that only excited me more. His dick flopped out of his boxers and that was like a runner hearing a gun at the start of a race. It had been

Main Chick vs Side Bitch

forever since I was eye level to a dick and his was plump and long, already hard.

"Yeah…I'm just about to leave the shop…" I slide him in my mouth, tasting every part of him thinking about every dollar that I needed for my daughter. Yeah I'm turned on by DeWayne but money makes me come more.

But he didn't turn me away, I knew I still had what it took to get a man.

Slobbing on his dick, letting the head hit the back of my throat I thought about what things were about to be like as my life as his side bitch. I had been here before, shit my baby daddy was married when I was with him so I knew the game. Taking his dick out and sucking his balls and twisting his dick in my hands was when I heard his voice crack.

He grabbed a fist full of my hair and that's when I knew it. I was going to have more money than I knew what to do with and in no time my daughter would be back home. Side bitches always win and as he talked to his other bitch on the phone I didn't feel no guilt for that hoe as I took her man's dick deep into my jaw.

7

Kiara

I was driving through the dark streets on autopilot with no memory or recognition of anything. It was a miracle I made it home in one piece because I didn't remember any stop lights, street signs, or cars but before I knew it I was at my condo my hands squeezing the steering wheel with my mind twirling.

What would my mother think and what would my father have said if they were here? I wasn't sure but I could see them both saying, do whatever it is you must to survive.

Both of my parents were hard workers, going to work everyday to send me to private school and put me in the best programs.

Before they died that's all they talked about and my mother especially vocal and drilling it into my head how far I must push to be the best.

"Kiara you must work twice as hard as the next person. Do what they won't do."

She might not have meant that I sleep with my boss to become partner but doing what I had to meant so many things.

After they died when I was fifteen, I had to do a lot of things I didn't want to do. Working a full time job through high school. While all the other kids went home, I headed to a burger joint to wash dishes and work the cash register.

When other people had their parents taking pictures at graduation, I had no one there. Instead of partying that night I went back to work because I had college to pay for.

That hurt, I still cried thinking about my friends going to graduation parties thrown by their parents but instead my parents were in the ground.

Then when I got to college it was more work, studying for hours then holding down a job so I didn't have to take out student loans. It was rough, everyday was filled with obstacles and pitfalls of things I didn't want to do.

Mr. Puzder was just like those jobs, he was those late nights of studying, he was the trips to the soup kitchens so I could save money, he was everything I didn't want to conquer for my success. And just like each of those things, I did it, got over it, and won.

Yet, now I still felt guilty and dirty like some street walking prostitute after a night on the track. But I didn't get paid like a prostitute; there wasn't one bitch on the street that was degraded like me. I doubted there were prostitutes that graduated Magnum Cum Laude of their undergrad and law school class. And unlike them I wasn't on any type of drugs and there was no pimp in my pockets or putting his foot up my ass. I rationalized it all, making myself feel more normal for doing what I did with Mr. Puzder in the presidential suite.

I was a self made woman and sometimes you have to do things that you don't want to, and fucking Puzder was just business. My parents died when I was young but they groomed me even younger and it all paid off now. This was life, making sacrifices, and I was cool with that as long as I made partner and credentials were behind my name.

Before I left the suite, Puzder guaranteed that I would be partner and of course, I pressed record on my cell phone and played it back for him. He assured me that it wasn't necessary for any kind of black mail because he would stand by his word.

I believed him; especially since I was going to make sure that he stuck to what he promised.

Once I was in his room the deed was easy, I simply went somewhere else.

I wasn't fucking Puzder, I simply convinced myself it was DeWayne inside me and not some old man with gray hair. I could take my mind wherever I wanted it to go and when I got home I just wanted to take a shower and lay in my man's arms.

I didn't realize that DeWayne wasn't home until I got in the house. Everything in the condo was the way I left it that morning with not one thing moved.

It was close to twelve now, and usually by this time he would be home but of course he was probably out with some bitch.

This was the shit that I didn't deserve, I talked till I was fucking hoarse with DeWayne about wanting him home but even though I was late he still wasn't here yet.

The first thing that came to my mind was our conversation earlier when I found out I paid for my own damn engagement ring.

I turned on my phone calling him, he answered but I could tell something was wrong.

"When are you coming home?"

"Oh, I'm leaving the shop now." It sounded like a lie. He was good as a barber but there was no one that was getting their hair cut this late at night but I didn't have the energy to argue. Instead I told him okay and stripped off every piece of clothing and got into the shower.

With the hot water running over my body, I had a million thoughts running through my mind.

Maybe me being partner would change my relationship with DeWayne. Maybe he would finally see that I was way better than these whores that he had this crazy fascination for.

I would be making twice as much as I am now, I could afford to get the shop expanded. We could open the boutiques he talked about and get him from behind the barber chair and into another position.

I had so many plans for our careers and for our personal lives that would now be able to happen, only if I could get DeWayne to realize them.

I stayed in the shower until the water turned cold, washing myself until my fingers turned to prunes but there was still no DeWayne.

I waited up for him like a good little fiancé with our forty six inch television on but I wasn't looking at the tube. I just wanted him home, I wanted to wrap my arms around him and let him tell me he loved me. I just needed to feel some type of love tonight.

But as soon as I heard his key in the door and felt his presence in the house, I knew it.

I could smell the pussy on him as he walked through the door.

"How was the basketball game?" I didn't wait, I didn't give him time to take off his coat or his shoes I just went right in. He told me that he wasn't going with me because of his son's basketball game and it just registered that he told me he was leaving the shop when I called.

I guess he must have cloned himself because how could he be in two places at one time.

"Hey babe. How was your night? Oh, mine was fine. Thanks...the fuck is wrong with you?" He had an attitude, that was my second clue. Usually when he was doing something wrong he had the nerve to try to be mad at me. But what could I say to that. *It was good babe. I had to fuck my boss just so I could make partner all because you weren't there to escort me to the meeting.*

"I'm more worried about your night…" I watched him as he got undressed, throwing his clothes into the hamper.

"Whatever, man. I'm not about to argue with you. I had a long night." He went into the bathroom, slamming the door behind him.

I smelled his clothes as the shower came on in the bathroom. He didn't smell like hairspray like usual, it was cheap perfume.

I waited with his shirt in my hands until he was done, coming out dripping in water with a towel around his waist like nothing was wrong.

"Tell that bitch to change her perfume." I threw the shirt in his face.

"Man, what the fuck are you on?"

"That bitch smells like some cheap bullshit you buy from the drug store. Tell her if she is going to compete with me she needs to step it up." I grabbed one of my designer perfumes off the dresser.

"Here, tell her she should be on some shit like this. These cost me one hundred and fifty dollars a bottle." I didn't realize I was so mad until the bottle went sailing across the room, hitting the wall and crashing into pieces.

"WHAT THE FUCK IS WRONG WITH YOU." He screamed dodging out of the way. He pulled clothes out of the closet, sliding on shorts.

"No. Ain't shit wrong with me but you. You're lying, you're cheating, and here I am selling my soul for you."

That's what I felt like, I was working and doing all of these things to make this man happy but what did he do for me.

"Man, I'm getting the fuck out of here." He was dressed in a flash, grabbing his coat and zipping it up. "Fuck if I come over here and you're on some crazy shit." I didn't have a chance to say a word before he grabbed his eyes and flew out the door.

I wanted to stop him, tell him I was having one of the worst days of my life and that I was sorry but I couldn't say any of that without telling him the truth. Then he would be pissed at me, I would be the one in the wrong but after all of the bitches he has fucked around on me with I hadn't even come close to evening the score.

"Wait…" I screamed after him, hoping he would hear me but instead I heard a few fast beeps followed by a buzzing noise from his cell phone on the nightstand. The lawyer and side of me was begging to take a look and see who was calling.

Opening his phone the name Ariane was there. The bitch from the shop, the hair braiding bitch who he got so upset about.

Her text message was short but I had no idea what the fuck she sent it for especially this late at night

"Thank you :)"

WHAT THE FUCK was she thanking him for? I looked through their messages only but I didn't get far when I heard the door opening and footsteps rushing towards the room.

"I forgot my phone." He was in the bedroom before I could pretend like I wasn't being a snoop. Now on top of being mad at me had had caught me doing the thing he hated this most, that was go through his personal belongings...especially his phone.

Snatching it from my hand he didn't say a word as he stepped over the glass and dripping perfume that was now suffocating the room. Seconds later a hard slam of the door solidified it for me, he wasn't going to apologize.

Opening the window, the cold breeze filled the room instantly as I started cleaning the war zone. My room was a mess, and my life was even messier. The cold air took away some of the smell of my perfume that was usually a pleasant fragrance but an entire bottle was too much and almost made me want to throw up.

I should have aimed for his head, now I was left grabbing the vacuum and trying to get glass out of my carpet.

As the vacuum roared through the room my mind started turning.

What did this bitch have to thank my man for at twelve o'clock at night? Was he fucking her already? The bitch looked easy or maybe he was fucking some other bitch.

I was so tired of him cheating, all these hoes tempting and pulling my man in a million different directions when I was the only bitch he needed.

You need to claim what's yours, I heard my Mom's voice in my head. She used to push me so much to get what I wanted, take no prisoners, and give no fucks about anyone's feelings.

I finished vacuuming trying to figure out what I could do with this chick but I knew nothing about this new employee, and that's when it hit me.

Turning off the vacuum, I went to my laptop and logged on to the accounting software we had for the shop.

Whenever we hired somebody new, DeWayne had to file a tax form and send it in to the state board of Cosmetology.

He had to print that form from the accounting software so that's where I went, going down the list of past and present stylists until I found her name.

Ariane Collins

THAT WAS ALL I NEEDED. A first and last name was more than a good enough start for me. This time tomorrow I would know everything I needed to know about this bitch. Operation *Get Rid of the Side Hoes* was in full effect.

8

Ariane

I was dreaming about him, going over how he plunged his dick deep inside me. Twisting me on the bed and pushing my head into a pillow while I tooted my ass up to him.

I screamed his name, calling him daddy over and over again until knocking came crashing into my bedroom and my dream faded away.

"Ariane it's me..." I heard him yelling but I had to still be dreaming. Jumping from the bed ,I grabbed a robe and shuffled to the door only to look through the peep hole and see DeWayne.

I opened the door, quickly letting him in and quickly shutting the door behind him.

"What the hell is going on? What are you doing back here?" I was glad he was back, but it was three in the morning and I had to be right back up for a seven o'clock appointment.

"I just...man I've been out riding around thinking about shit." He walked deeper into my apartment and sitting down on the couch. "I just can't believe what went down earlier Shorty and I haven't been able to get you out of my head."

Was this nigga serious, the dick was good but I sent him home to his chick. Truthfully, I did the shit just to show that tired ass hoe that she wasn't all that. Now this nigga was trying to be all lovey dovey.

"I mean, what you think. I'm tripping. I'm gonna leave." He stood up to go but I blocked his way. I still didn't want him to leave and maybe this was a good thing.

"Naw...I'm just shocked like. I thought you and the lawyer lady…"

"Man...I don't even want to talk about her." He moved closer to me, his cold hands pulling back my robe revealing my nakedness.

"I just want to think about you and me," he whispered as he nibbled on my ear. "I been wanting this since I met you," he said pulling me close, my body trembling in his hands.

I said I only wanted the money, some dick, and eventually I would just move on but this man was fine as hell.

Maybe prison hadn't made me as hard as I thought I was because as we kissed, I felt butterflies take flight in my stomach.

It was too late, as much as I was trying to fight it. This nigga had me wet, horny, and probably somewhat in love with his ass. All within one week.

*****

DEWAYNE WAS MORE of a man than I thought he was. In the last week, he had turned my entire life around. He gave me the money I needed to pay my lawyer, pushing more and more customers my way, and every night he has been at my house breaking me off the best dick I have ever had.

Now today, bright and early at the shop I was looking at my man with a few clients waiting and a serious look etched in his face as he cut hair. He was about his business and everything in life was good, especially since I haven't heard shit from Ms. lawyer bitch.

He hasn't said her name and I haven't asked any questions but everyday I came to the shop in my tennis shoes and my hair pulled back ready to fight this bitch. I wasn't even the type to fight no bitch over no man but with how good his dick was and how much I was falling for this nigga, I would have went up against all the dykes in prison for DeWayne.

There was a smile on my face that couldn't be removed since me and DeWayne started on this road together and as I parted my client's hair ready to start another braid I heard a loud beeping of a truck backing up.

Looking outside I thought I was seeing things and before I could move my mouth to speak, DeWayne was already screaming.

"Oh shit...they towing my car." He dropped his clippers so fast and flew out the door and I was right behind him, right along with every other nosy motherfucker in the shop.

"YO! Why you towing my shit?" he yelled at the tow truck operator. A fat sloppy ass dude flopped out of the tow truck showing DeWayne some papers.

I couldn't hear what they were saying but DeWayne's hands were moving as a stiff cold breeze moved across the parking lot.

People were whispering shit and laughing, I wanted to tell all of they ass to shut the fuck up until a car pulled right up on the parking lot with the speakers blaring blocking our view of DeWayne and the tow truck.

"Tell that motherfucker to move." I screamed. I took a step closer as the door opened and I saw the devil herself, little Ms. Lawyer bitch coming out smiling like the damn devil.

"What the fuck is going on Kiara? Why you towing my shit?" I shook my head, the bitch couldn't have him so she was going to take back all of her shit like a petty bitch. I took a step forward, ready to say something.

"Baby...why you worried about that old truck when you got a new Benz?" Her words hit me and I was confused until she stepped back and presented the car to DeWayne.

"Yo...you serious. This is mine?" I looked at the car more closely. It had to be brand new with temporary plates, tinted windows, and custom black rims making the car look fierce.

DeWayne ran his hand across the car and without even looking my way he did the most disrespectful shit I had ever seen.

Pulling the bitch close, he kissed her right in front of me, and not no peck on the cheek but a full-fledged tongue rolling kiss.

I stepped around the car only to see him grabbing her ass like he was about to fuck her in the parking lot.

"Go ahead, take it for a drive." She said handing him the keys.

"Damn right...thanks baby. Thank you so much." The tow truck driver continued his job, towing away DeWayne's truck as he slide in the Benz and backed off the parking lot.

Little Ms. Lawyer turned to me as DeWayne pulled away, a stare down that I had been waiting for but I didn't imagine the shit was going to go down like this.

Looking back, everybody was back in the shop now, they were probably used to this rich ass bitch and her antics but all this bullshit made me sick.

DeWayne rolled up and down the street as Ms. Lawyer bitch starred at me, finally after a half a minute she spoke.

"Your name is Ariane, right."

"Yeah, why?"

"Ariane Collins?" She asked stepping to me with a smile on her face and extending her hand. I wasn't sure how this bitch knew my whole name but I shook her pathetic ass hand.

"Well it's nice to put a name with a face. I think we got off on the wrong foot the last time I saw you. I'm Kiara, the co-owner of the shop and DeWayne's fiancé." She wiggled a ring in my face like I gave a fuck. Only if she knew her fiancé was at my crib for the last week fucking my brains out. Where was she when he was calling my name and pulling my hair all in my bed for the last seven days?

"And...what the fuck is that supposed to mean?" She only laughed at my question.

"Well, I just thought we should get to know each other. Since you are new here and I am sort of like your boss you know." She laughed but I didn't see shit funny. "Hopefully we can be friends. I'm sure you need all the friends you can get. You know with your custody case and all." I felt like a bowling ball had be dropped on my stomach. All air left my body as I looked in this bitch's face.

Her smile faded as she continued to speak.

"I know you have been fucking my man and that's cool. Believe me, you aren't the first and you probably won't be the last. But you see that's my man and soon to be my husband." DeWayne rolled down the street yet another time, burning rubber as the bitch kept talking.

"He is an adventurer, he has this thing for little bitches like you which are a dime a dozen. But you see...a bitch like me is a once in a lifetime." I didn't have the words to say to this hoe. My hand clenched and I was ready to hit her right in her fucking forehead but I let her talk.

"You see, I know you have a case coming up. The custody of your daughter. Your baby is six years old right? Little Avianna is so precious." She knew my baby's name and the bitch was laughing about it.

"How the fuck do you know my daughter…" But she cut me off.

"Bitch, I know everything under the motherfucking sun and I know that if you don't leave DeWayne alone, your not going to ever know what it feels like to have custody of your daughter again." She stepped closer to me, our faces so close that we were almost touching each other.

The bitch was starring me down when DeWayne pulled back into the parking lot.

He jumped out the car quicker than Superman and tried stepping between us.

"Yo yo..what's going on here baby?" But he wasn't talking to me. He was talking to Ms. Lawyer bitch.

"Oh nothing boo. I was just introducing myself to Ariane." She laughed straightening out her suit. "It was nice meeting you Ms. Collins and welcome to Cutting Edge." The bitch was trying to be funny but I was so mad I felt like crying.

DeWayne didn't even look at me, he pulled her off to the side with his hand around her waist and his back to me.

That told me what it was, this nigga was a bitch and he didn't give a fuck about me. As bad as I wanted to fuck him and this hoe up I had to think rational.

If she knew this much about me and my baby, that

meant that she could fuck my whole world up and DeWayne and his dick weren't worth Avianna not being with her mother.

I turned around, going back into the shop and all eyes were on me. It wasn't a mystery that me and DeWayne were fucking but up until today I thought it was a good thing, now as I walked back to my station I felt like the shop fool.

I held back my tears, smiling for my client like nothing was wrong but inside I was ready to kill a motherfucker.

I watched as another car arrived, some black tinted town car.

DeWayne gave the lawyer bitch a kiss and opened the back door for her and helped her inside.

She was right, I didn't have that type of money. He was a bitch ass nigga for claiming he wanted to be with me and he was through with her but now he was kissing her ass.

When he stepped back in the shop, I didn't even look his way. Instead, I kept repeating the number three to myself over and over again. That was how many days I had until I got my daughter back. Right now, that was the only thing that mattered. Not no cheating ass nigga, not no rich lawyer bitch, but my daughter Avianna. She was the only thing I had left in this world.

9

DeWayne

"Dawg, I heard yo wifey bossed up on you today." I was in my new whip, talking to my brother on the hands free system. Somehow everybody in the hood knew about my new Benz and what Keke did.

"That's why she is my bottom bitch nigga. She always come through and know how to treat a nigga." I was on my way home to her right now. After a long day at the shop I was usually tired but tonight I couldn't wait to get off and get back into my brand new car that my baby bought me.

The last time I saw Keke she was throwing bottles of perfume at a nigga and today I thought she was on some bullshit but instead she was on some boss shit. I loved that bitch with all my heart for doing this.

"Man, you a sucka for money ass nigga." My brother laughed but I didn't see no bitches pulling up to his job with no new cars.

"Whatever nigga. I'm at the crib I'll hit you later."

"Aight." I hung up on him right from the steering

wheel as I pulled into the condo. I hadn't been back in a week and it felt good to finally be back home.

Being at Ariane's was cool but Keke knew how to treat a nigga. From the shit she bought me, to her cooking, and her pussy fit my dick just right.

Everything was proper and as I hopped out my new Benz I felt like a new man as I walked towards our condo.

"Honey, I'm home." I screamed as I used my key. This house was the place I felt most at home besides at my mom's crib.

"I'm in the bedroom." The smell of a home cooked meal hit me as I walked through the house meeting my queen in the bedroom.

"What you doing baller?" I joked with her picking her up. "What the hell was all that about?" We kissed as I pulled her in close. I wanted to ask her earlier but I was too busy trying to keep the peace between her and Ariane.

And it was no mystery that Keke had money and some good ass credit so whatever she wanted to buy she could get it.

"Well...I was waiting to tell you this but I made partner." the dollar signs were calculating in my head.

"Damn babe, you serious?" I picked her up twirling her around the room.

"Yeah boo. We can do all the things we ever wanted. I'm sorry about last week." She poked her lip out wrapping her arms around me.

"Babe...don't worry about that shit alright. We just gotta stick it out whatever we got going on." Especially since she was now a partner at one of the most prestigious law firms in the city. Shit, it might be one of the most prestigious in the country.

"Baby, I just want this to be a fresh start for us." I wanted the same thing too, if she wasn't asking no questions then I wasn't saying shit about where I had been for the last week.

"So what you wanna do boo? You wanna go celebrate?" I twirled her around, she laughed and giggled but she stopped me and sat me down.

"More than anything DeWayne I want us to take advantage of this opportunity. We need to get more shops." I rolled my eyes at that shit.

"That's a lot of work Ke. I'm not going to be able to cut hair if I'm doing all that." And that's when she smiled.

"That's my point. You need to switch up what your doing. And that includes fucking these hoes." Shit...I hoped she didn't turn this shit into an argument.

"Baby, we can talk about all of that. Whatever you wanna do I'm wit it. But I'm proud of you girl." That was the truth. I had seen Keke work her ass off at the firm and now she was partner. A young black woman was partner and she was my woman.

"Baby, I want to go ahead and get married and take this thing to the next level." My heart shook when she said that. I thought about my baby momma's and how they would act if I got married. They didn't know I was engaged, shit I didn't even tell them tricks I was with anybody. The less they knew the better.

"Boo we can handle all that. Look here, tonight we are going to celebrate. Go ahead and change so we can go out." I felt like taking my baby out for a spin. And I meant the new Benz and Keke needed to go out and be seen.

"For real boo. Shit I gotta take a shower."

"Well go ahead girl. Go get in and make it quick."

"Okay." She smiled from ear to ear giving me a kiss and jumping up to go to the bathroom but her purse fell over knocking everything on the floor.

"It's cool, I got it boo. Go ahead and get ready." She

smiled at that as I bent down to pick up the contents of her purse.

It was the same shit every chick has in her purse. Lipstick, car keys and a wallet but the last thing laying on the floor was a card. Looking at it closer, I saw it wasn't just no card but a motherfucking hotel key.

The water was already running in the shower and I could hear her shutting the shower doors but I didn't give a fuck. I wanted to know what this shit was.

"Yo, when you ever been to the Grand Laury Hotel?" I asked her showing her the room key through the shower glass doors.

"Aww babe. That was from Tisha's bachelorette party. You know her and Tony are going to Vegas and getting married this weekend." I was pissed, ready to explode until she reminded me of that.

"Aww okay. That's wassup?"

Her phone ringing cut into our conversation.

"Baby can you answer that for me." I did as she said going to her phone back in the bedroom and answering.

"Hey wassup DeWayne. Where my girl at?" Speak of the devil it was Tisha, the only one of Keke's friends that I actually thought was cool.

"She in the shower T. Congrats on the wedding I almost forgot you was about to tie the knot."

"Thanks hun...when you gonna make it official with my girl?" She laughed and it made me wish I would have never answered the phone.

"Shit, I don't know. If you have her a bachelorette party like yours then I don't know if we getting married." I laughed but Tisha was quiet as a church mouse. The line went silent like she hung up.

"Hello?"

"Yeah...I mean I don't believe in bachelorette parties." I looked at the key still in my hand.

"So you didn't have nothing at the Grand Laury? Keke told me..." Before I could get the whole sentence out Tisha was cutting me off.

"Oh yeah...my bad bruh I thought you meant bridal shower or something. Yeah we had a super time." Something didn't sound right but the shower went off and I heard Keke getting out.

"Aight then, here ya go, your friend." I handed Keke the phone still with the room key in my hand.

Something didn't feel right and the shit damn sure didn't sound right.

Tisha was a nurse, she didn't just forget shit and she damn sure heard everything I said but I didn't say shit. I pulled out the Benz keys in my pocket starring at them motherfuckas and thinking about all the shit me and Keke had been through.

She wouldn't dare cheat on you, I told myself and I prayed that shit was true. Because if this bitch had me out here looking crazy I was gonna kill her ass. And I meant that shit from the bottom of my heart.

10

Ariane

I was nervous sitting in the courtroom as my lawyer, Mr. Fabri, argued my case for me. My baby daddy Paul sat on the other side in a suit and tie, the motherfucka couldn't even look at me.

"Your honor, my client has exhibited excellent recover since her release from prison. She is gainfully employed, she has a residence in a stable environment." My lawyer was speaking the truth. Everything that I was supposed to be doing I did it and all within six months of getting out of prison. Now I wanted my daughter back.

I sat up straight dressed in a suit with my hair down over my shoulders, looking like an innocent church member ready for Sunday school. I would have dressed like a kindergarten teacher if it meant I could have my little girl at home with me.

"Council, what do you have to say about Ms. Collins regaining her rights?" I turned to see Paul's lawyer stand up.

"Your honor, the child has been living with my client for the last five years." I wanted to object, tell the court that the reason why I went to jail was covering Paul's ass. Since I've been locked up he's changed into a corporate man and no longer the dope dealer he was when I went in. But now he wanted to keep me away from my daughter like I was the fucked up person. "You see the child is comfortable, in a stable school district and home schedule and we feel uprooting the child at this time is counter productive to her development." I rolled my eyes at that bullshit. What was counterproductive was keeping her away from her mother. Restricting my time to parent only on the weekends and every other Wednesday was straight bullshit.

"Judge we disagree…" My lawyer stood up ready to challenge but the judge struck his gavel against the wooden desk.

"I've already made a ruling in this I don't need any further testimony." My heart was beating so fast I felt it in my throat.

"The child will hereby remain with the custodial parent for the time of one year when we will review this matter again. Court adjourned." He hit the gavel again as we stood but I didn't understand what happened.

"I'm sorry Ms. Collins, we will try this again next year." My lawyer told me but there was no next year. I had waited five years to be in my daughter's life and now that I was finally free he was still standing in my way.

"You son of a bitch...why can't I be her mother." I yelled across the courtroom at Paul. He shook his head at me as my lawyer pulled me back.

"Your wife is not her mother...I am her mother you punk bitch." If I was a nigga I would have beat his ass. Stomped him out in the courtroom until his blood covered the linoleum floor.

"Ms. Collins please get a hold of yourself. The judge

may take your right completely if you cause a scene." I didn't say another word. Instead, I grabbed my purse and left the courtroom not bothering to look back.

Through the halls, I damn near ran until I finally got to the door and down the courthouse steps. I just wanted to get to my car where I could cry without anyone seeing me.

I couldn't believe after all this time and after everything I've done to get her back, my baby still wasn't coming home.

As soon as I got in the car and closed the door the tears started to fall. I couldn't help it, down my cheeks like waterfalls I cried as I started the car.

I didn't want Paul coming out of the courthouse and having the satisfaction to see me cry after all the shit I have been through over him.

I didn't snitch, I didn't mention one word about him or his partners. Instead I went to prison losing years of my life and years in my daughter's life while he and his dick-gobbling wife raised my daughter.

The shit made my stomach turn, my skin felt hot like the sun was only a few feet away from me. I had to leave this area or I was going to do some shit that I wouldn't be able to come back from.

Pulling out of the parking space I sped down the street, only stopping because cars and a red light were blocking me in.

Wiping my face, I looked around hoping nobody was watching me cry in my car like a lunatic when I saw her.

Ms. Lawyer bitch was waiting at the intersection talking to some other bitch in a suit that looked just like her. I watched her like she was some fucking hologram and wasn't real, there was no way she was turning up just now at a time like this. But as I watched, she turned her head looking right at me.

For a moment, our eyes locked on each other and at first I didn't think she recognized me but then she smiled. She couldn't have been smiling at me, the same bitch that said that stupid shit outside the shop the other day.

She walked across the street, right in front of my car and the bitch had the nerve to wave, but the part that pissed me off the most was when she winked. I wanted to turn my wheel, put my foot on the gas and run the rich bitch and her friend over but that's when it hit me.

It was her fault, this was all her doing.

YOU KNOW with your custody case and all.

HER WORDS RANG in my ears and even as the light changed I couldn't move. It took all the cars behind me to honk for me to pull and move away from the light.

All because the bitch couldn't keep her man under control, she had to come fuck with me and my baby. Since the bullshit with the car and the shit she said, I hadn't even talked to DeWayne. I was done with it, we could make money together but I was done fucking him. She could have his dusty ass but why put my daughter in this?

My hands gripped the steering wheel tight as I drove, trying to fight the urge with everything in me not to turn around and go beat the shit out of this lady.

Instead I drove slow, breathing deep not looking in my rearview mirror at that evil bitch.

It was one thing to be mad at me, curse me out, even try to fight me but to involve my child was some next level shit.

My phone rang as I stopped at another light and as

much as I didn't want to talk I heard a ringtone that was music to my ears, it meant Avianna was calling.

I scrambled through my purse for my phone picking up and hearing her voice made me start crying all over again.

"Mommy, I made a bracelet for you." I couldn't hold it in, I managed to pull over, crying, trying not to make too much noise as my baby spoke to me.

"Oh that's nice baby."

"Mommy, when am I going to see you." I felt like dying, right here in the middle of the day I just wanted to ball myself up and die. I missed and loved this little girl so much and I wanted to see her way more than I was allowed to.

"Mommy will see you next Wednesday baby." I tried not to choke as I attempted to talk without sounding like the crying mess that I was. It was hard to explain to a child about next Wednesday when they were five.

"How many days is that?" She was so smart, always asking me these questions.

"Just three more baby girl. Can you count to three for Mommy?"

"Of course Mommy…One…Tew…" She was so cute, her little voice coming through the phone had me going as we counted together. "And then theee"

"Yep your right. That's Mommy's smart girl. Just three days." This hurt like hell. It hurt more than getting locked away because I wasn't free to roam around but now that I was out and still away from her, I felt like death.

"Okay Mommy, I love you."

"I love you too baby."

"Bye bye…" she said bye and we hung up. The bastard Paul must have had his bitch of a wife tell Avianna to call me. That was the least that he could do but I would deal with his ass one day. Eventually he will feel everything that

I felt and so would the Ms. Lawyer bitch. She had fucked with the wrong one, keeping me from my baby.

I merged back on the road thinking of my baby and how this bitch had fucked me over when I had the perfect idea.

"Dammit Ariane you smart crazy bitch…I think you have a brilliant plan." I congratulated myself as soon as the idea hit my thoughts.

"If that bitch is going to keep you from your seed. Maybe you should just have another one with her man." I laughed so hard I almost swerved and hit a car. But the plan was brilliant.

I didn't know when, and I didn't know exactly how to make it happen but DeWayne was going to give me a baby.

"I'll see how you play with people's kids then bitch when you're paying me child support." I laughed so hard I cried but this time instead of tears of sadness I was crying tears of joy. I had just thought of the ultimate payback and this way, nobody had to die.

11

DeWayne

I was spending my night at a party to celebrate my girl-becoming partner but right now I felt like I was at an execution. These people were killing me with their bullshit and stupid ass conversation.

I had on a suit because Keke demanded I put one on but I didn't give a fuck about impressing these rich motherfuckas. So instead of mingling I stayed over by the bar, counting the seconds until ten o'clock because that was exactly when I told her we were leaving.

But instead of being able to drink my vodka in peace I was having this awkward ass conversation with one of her bosses.

"So your Kiara's fiance, correct?" This dude Mr. Puzder was the best example for an uncle Tom ass nigga that I have ever seen.

He was in front of me drinking a gin and tonic. I have never seen a nigga drink a gin and tonic and he talked like he was a white boy that sprayed himself black.

I instantly didn't like this motherfucka, from the moment Kiara introduced him to me and when I tried to get away and get a drink at the bar he seemed to follow me like the motherfucka wanted to be my friend.

"Yeah, that's my baby."

"Hmmm...and what is it that you do?" This motherfucka was nosy. I sipped my vodka before I answered this motherfucka as I tried not to say some crazy shit.

"I'm an entrepreneur. I own a salon and apparel store..." He started laughing before I got my sentence out.

"Ohhh I admire little small business owners like you. The balls of a walrus but the brain of a dinosaur." Did this motherfucka just call me stupid?

I looked around for Kiara, because either this motherfucka was drunk or he was a straight up bitch. Either way, I was ready to go.

There were so many people in the ballroom that it was hard for me to find Kiara but I finally saw her. Somehow she looked my way just as I was looking at her way.

"Well, you do have to have big nuts to go after your dreams." I gulped down my vodka, standing tall and fixing my suit as Kiara walked over with another woman.

"Ms. Puzder this is my fiancee DeWayne."

"Ohh so nice to meet you. I know you are proud of your leading lady here." The sister seemed too down to earth to be with this clown ass nigga. I pulled Kiara close as I answered the dick head's wife while he stood looking stupid.

"Well yes, it is a very proud moment when a strong woman like Kiara reaches such an accomplishment." The Mr. Puzder motherfucka laughed a little bit but his wife ignored it.

"That's nice. So when are you two getting married?" Kiara looked at me but she opted to answer that question.

"I'm thinking when I finally get my case load under control so probably in the next six months."

"Have you picked a location?"

"Ummm no, not yet." Hell no we hadn't picked a location because I wasn't ready to get married, I didn't say that but of course the Puzder motherfucka had to say something.

You should get married at the Grand Laury hotel. Lovely place." I had heard of that place but I couldn't remember where I heard it.

"Oh yes, Chris just took me there for our twentieth anniversary last week." Kiara started coughing as she said that and the Puzder dude looked like he wanted to laugh.

"It's a beautiful place. Be sure to check there for sure."

"What is the name again?" I asked them trying to remember where I saw it.

"Its the Grand Laury Hotel. Downtown it's a huge building with an AMAZING view." I ran through my brain trying to remember and it came to me.

That was the same name of the hotel from that key I found in Kiara's purse.

"Yep, me and the wife have been going for years. It's my favorite place, you two should get married there. Right Kiara." She wasn't talking, she was too busy shaking her head and sipping her wine.

"Well, it's getting late Mr. and Mrs. Puzder. We're going to slide on out." She shook both of their hands and I watched as she got to him, how he held Kiara's hand just a few seconds longer than he should have.

How his eyes searched over her body was some weird shit.

"Nice meeting you Deraye," he mispronounced my name, I wanted to punch his bitch ass but I kept it nice.

"It's DeWayne."

"Oh yeah...sorry." He smiled but he wasn't sorry. He

gave me a handshake and I squeezed his hand back just as hard as he squeezed mine.

"Got a good handshake there. You know your fiance likes a good shake." I thought I heard him wrong, he said the shit so low that I thought I was hearing things.

"What you say?" He didn't repeat it. Instead, he grabbed his wife and walked away as I followed Kiara out the ballroom and down a hall towards valet.

As she talked about the night, my mind was doing fucking cartwheels over what I just heard him say.

YOU KNOW your fiance likes a good shake.

"BABY, do you have the valet ticket?" She smiled but I didn't find shit funny. I handed her the ticket as I watched her. Thinking of how just a week ago she had a key to the same hotel that the motherfucka was talking about. She never mentioned him but now he was an expert in everything about us and talking to me like he knew some shit about me.

"So is your boss always like that?" She froze when I asked her about him.

"What do you mean?"

"An asshole, a dickhead, a bitch...is he always like that?" She shook her head.

"No, he's just being funny." She laughed and I didn't once again as the valet pulled up with the car.

I got in the driver side of my Benz and the valet closed the passenger door for Kiara.

I sped off the lot, not burning rubber but damn close.

"What's wrong?" I didn't feel well, something wasn't right and I was going to get to the bottom of the shit.

"Some shit don't feel right." I told her as I hopped on the highway pushing my new car to eighty miles an hour.

"C'mon with that shit DeWayne, you do this every time I try to take you somewhere."

"No the fuck I don't"

"You never wanna do anything with me so you always get this dumb ass madness going on." I was pissed but I wasn't imagining this shit.

"Yeah, you would be the same way." I told her as I made my way home not even wanting to go over this in the car. I sped faster as she shut up and I turned on the music.

The louder the radio was, the clearer my thoughts came at me.

The fact that he was talking about that hotel to all the other little remarks he made but the last one took the cake.

We got home in record time, pulling into the parking lot. I was about to get out but I stopped Kiara before she got set both of her feet out the door.

"Has he tried something with you?"

"Come on DeWayne what the fuck?" I didn't understand why she was getting so mad.

"Did he?"

"No...he is..."

"TELL ME THE FUCKING TRUTH!" I know what I felt and I felt that something wasn't right.

"You don't have to yell I told you..." I got out of the car before she could finish her lie. Slamming the door, I opened the door to the apartment in record time.

"Look, don't be slamming the car..." I grabbed her ass as she came into the house, slamming her back against the front door.

"DID YOU FUCK HIM?"

"No..."

"No? Then what the fuck did he mean you like to be shaken?"

"What...I" I shook her ass, right there in the living room door I shook her as hard as I could.

"Stop it, your hurting me."

"DID YOU FUCK HIM!" I screamed at her, squeezing her shoulders.

She didn't say a word, she just looked at me. The tears filling her eyes and I knew that moment and at that second that she had sex with that smug motherfucka.

"DAMMIT Kiara...DAMN!" I punched at the wall, the drywall folding under my fist but it was better than punching her.

"I'm sorry..." She was crying, sliding down the wall to the floor as I paced back and forth ready to punch another wall.

"I didn't mean." I threw a vase against the wall. Flowers and water crashing to the wall shutting her up.

"I'm leaving." I wasn't dealing with this shit.

"Wait baby...we can talk about this."

"AIN'T SHIT TO TALK ABOUT!" I screamed at her, pushing her to the side as she tried to grab me. I walked out the door.

In my suit and all, I walked to my car, got in and pulled out before I fucked her up.

"FUCK!" I screamed to the car, punching the steering wheel.

Bitches can't do what we do, especially not to a nigga like me. I sailed down the road wanting to fuck somebody up. My main chick wasn't my main no more, she had fucked somebody else and I was ready to kill a motherfucka over it.

No matter how many bitches I fucked, Kiara's pussy

belonged to me and she had broken the cardinal rule. Don't ever give my pussy away...I always told her that.

This was a fucked up night and as I gripped the wheel I knew only one thing was going to help me get over this shit. And that was more pussy.

12

Ariane

I hadn't smoked any weed since I went to prison but now, in my living room in the middle of the night I was lighting up. I sat in the dark in a long t-shirt puffing a joint and filling the air with smoke.

I had to do something to calm my nerves or I was going to hurt somebody.

I had turned my phone off when I got home from court not wanting to be disturb but as I puffed on the joint I heard knocks at the door.

I wasn't expecting anybody, nobody ever came to visit me but looking through the peephole it was DeWayne.

I opened the door for him, not expecting to see him until tomorrow.

"Wassup." I opened the door a crack but the fire in his eyes said it all.

I let him in as he paced through the living room.

I didn't even ask him what was going on, I just passed him the joint and waited for him to start talking.

After two long puffs he opened up, laying down everything that was going on.

How Kiara was fucking her boss, how he wasn't happy but was trying to make it work for the money and some other bullshit.

"I was gonna kill that bitch." He sounded crazy and I wanted to laugh at him. He was going to kill her for some shit that he did to her all the time.

"Why don't you just leave then DeWayne? Why do you keep doing this shit?" He passed me the joint and I began to puff as he pulled off his suit jacket.

He looked so handsome in his suit, it was a difference from the jeans and t-shirt he wore everyday.

"I just…"

"You know what. You kicked me to the curb for that bitch." I told him the truth as I got up and stood in his face. "I'm a down ass bitch and I would never do that to you." I was telling the truth and before I could finish talking he kissed me.

His tongue was in my mouth before I could take a breath.

"I want you. I fucked up. I don't want that bitch, I want you." That was exactly what I figured he would say. I doubted that he would come crawling back this soon but I had to always be prepared and I told myself I wasn't getting caught off guard anymore with anything.

"Aww yeah…then prove it." I pulled him to the room as he pulled at my shirt.

I did the work for him, pulling off the oversized shirt and revealing my bare ass to him.

"Damn girl." Through the moonlight peeping through the shades, I could see his dick was at attention in his pants.

I helped him, getting down on my knees to unbutton his pants and as soon as his dick popped out I put it in my mouth.

Sucking hard like my life depended on it. Grabbing his legs, I pushed his dick into the back of my throat and sucking with every bit of breath in me.

"Damn girl...you missed a nigga." A missed his ass a whole lot and I was just about to show him how much.

"Fuck me raw boo... I wanna feel all of you." I told him jumping up on the bed and tooting my wet ass in the air.

"Naw boo...we can't do that. I already got enough shorties." he was tugging on his dick and I knew a little bit more persuasion might sway him in my way or it could turn him off completely.

'Aight.." I didn't argue. Going to my nightstand I grabbed the condom that I prepared for a time like this.

He couldn't tell but in the gold packaging were small little needle holes, just a few to put holes in the condom but not too much to where he would notice.

I opened the package, slipping the condom down his dick as I twirled the head in my mouth.

"Damn girl...Shit…" he moaned and as soon as I had the condom all the way on, I bent over in front of him taking his dick and sliding inside my wet pussy.

As hard as he pushed into me I pushed back harder, praying with every stroke.

Please Lord, let him bust a nut in me so big that he gets me pregnant...please. I wasn't sure if the Lord heard my prayer but as he pushed, I pushed and when he moaned so did I.

I was going to fuck him and poke as many holes in these condoms as I had to in order to get pregnant by this man.

Little Ms. Lawyer bitch had fucked up. She had never met a bitch like me, a do anything go to war type bitch and what she did today was set this whole battle into play.

"You like that shit girl?" he asked me and of course I did.

"Hell yeah...give it to me baby. This is your pussy." I told him the truth, it was his pussy and in nine months a baby was going to be coming out of the same pussy he was fucking. One way or another I was going to have DeWayne's baby and his main bottom bitch was going to be taking care of all three of us. DeWayne, me, and our new child. The shit was so funny I wanted to laugh. Game on bitch...this would teach her to fuck with me.

To Be Continued...

**TEXT SOLAE
To
313131**

*For New Releases
and
Free Book Promos*

Part II

13

DeWayne

Momma's house was like my sanctuary. No matter what bitch I was with, when things got tough, I could always come back to Momma.

So this morning, instead of looking into Ariane's face, I was at Momma's crib getting some air and her home cooking.

No matter how early it was, Momma was always up and dressed. Her dress was perfectly pressed, and her long hair was twisted into a bun. Her jet black was fading, strings of white were invading her head, but she was aging gracefully. I missed the days of waking up to her cooking me breakfast, but back then she was screaming for me to get ready for school. Now, I was a grown man with a business and my own kids.

"When the last time you seen DJ and Deja?"

She must have been reading my thoughts as she scrambled more eggs and pulled bacon out of the oven.

"It's been a minute, Ma. They Momma is tripping." My baby momma, Didi, hadn't been the same since I broke up with her and turned her loose. Especially when she figured out that it was Keke buying the kids' clothes instead of me. She hated when I got with anybody who was better than her, and now she was making me and my family pay for it, especially Momma.

"I tried calling her, but she won't take my calls."

That pissed me off, but I kept eating. It was one thing to keep the kids away from me, but to keep them from their own grandmother was some spiteful bullshit. The bitch just wanted me to come over there and fuck her. If I did that, everything would be all right in the world.

Kiara said she was going to file the papers to get me custody, but that was before everything got fucked up between us.

"When you gonna settle down, boy, and have one of these fast tale heffas cook for you, instead of me?" Momma brought more bacon to the small kitchen table and piled it on my plate.

"You know they can't cook like you, Momma."

But the truth was, I didn't want to be around a chick every day. I tried that shit for the longest with Kiara and look what she did to me.

Now Ariane wanted the same thing. She was getting a little too clingy, so I had to let that shit go. Coming to Momma's was the best way for me to get some room; plus, I had a new hot thang I needed to take somewhere nobody would see us. Where better than Momma's basement? This would be the one place that Ariane would be too afraid to come checking up on me.

She knew Momma wouldn't play her trying to run up in her crib; that shit would be too disrespectful even for her hood ass.

Ariane was my main chick by default right now, and that meant that the big dog needed his space. She needed to know that sometimes the dog jumped the fence every once in a while.

"Slow down, chile. You eating like you were starving."

She was right. Pushing the pancakes into my mouth, I couldn't help it. Last night still had me tired.

"You know me, Ma. I love when you cook breakfast."

Pancakes, fried potatoes, bacon, and eggs were all piled on the table for me, but the slamming of the basement door made Momma turn around.

I told the bitch to be quiet when she left and to make sure to close the door quietly so Momma didn't hear, but sure enough, she heard the door slam.

"Who is that downstairs?"

As she looked out the window, I kept eating and pretended like I didn't hear her.

"Boy... You better answer me."

I still said nothing as I thought about how that bitch sucked me up last night. I wanted her to be gone before Momma woke up, but I couldn't keep her lips off my dick.

"DeWayne Sharief... Who is this girl walking down my driveway?"

"That's my friend, Ma." I left it at that, but of course, she wanted to know more.

"Your friend who you got in my house and didn't tell me?"

She always made me feel like a little boy when she went on this shit. I grabbed another pancake, trying to drown her out, but she kept going.

"Boy, you over there eating like you got another baby on the way."

That made me stop chewing. "Don't say that shit, Ma... You trying to jinx me?"

She almost made me want to leave, but I was still hungry. She might have been right—with all my other kids,

I ate like a released hostage when I had somebody pregnant.

"Boy, you already jinxed. Yo damn daddy's blood runs through you."

She was right about that. My daddy had more hoes than anybody I knew.

"Yeah remember when he said he had...more women than Macy's had dresses." I laughed but my momma didn't crack a smile. "C'mon, Ma. I know you're not still mad at him."

My Dad has been dead for years and Momma still refused to say his name. She brought him up only every now and then, but it was never in a positive way. It was always to tell me not to go down his road, but I couldn't help it if I was a ladies' man.

"No sir. I'm not mad at him," she said, stepping over to me and rubbing my head. "I'm just sorry I wasn't able to stop you from being like him."

"He wasn't that bad of a man. He did what he had to do. Only if he was still here…" I thought about my pops all the time, wishing I could talk to him about the shit I had going on, but he died years ago.

"Him not being here is his fault."

She sat down in the chair beside me. I hated when she got like this, just saying shit because she was bitter. I loved my Momma, but whatever happened between her and Pop was their business.

"Ma, I don't really wanna get into that. All that stuff was between y'all. Having a heart attack wasn't his fault."

"No, Son. There are things that you probably needed to know before now, but I never wanted to tell you."

She always said while I was growing up that it was his own fault that he was dead. Back then, I couldn't ask questions or tell Momma not to say something. Now that I was grown, I could tell her to leave Pop's name alone, but today she was insisting. As I pushed the last piece of pancake in my mouth, I was prepared to leave, because listening to this shit was not in my plans to start my day.

"You always say that it's his fault. How is a heart attack his fault, then?" I was listening, waiting for her to say something spiteful.

"Because he didn't die of a heart attack." She took a deep breath before continuing. "Your father died of AIDS."

I heard her words, but it didn't make sense. My daddy wasn't sick, coughing, or skinny with spots all over his face.

"Pop didn't have no AIDS... What are you…"

Before I could ask her, she got up from the table, walked to her room, and returned a minute later with a paper that she handed to me. At the top in bold letters it said, "Death Certificate."

"Look under cause of death."

My eyes scanned down, searching through the form until I found it:

Complications of Acquired Immune Deficiency Syndrome

"You see. That's why I'm telling you. The things that he said about women may have been fun at the time. All of the whoring around may have felt good, but look where it sent him. Straight to the cemetery."

I threw the form down, letting it fall on the floor. "No... You're lying!" I stood up, watching a tear fall from her face.

"I wouldn't lie to you, Son."

She had to be lying. There was no way my Pops died that way and I didn't know.

"We didn't want to tell you the truth, and I didn't want you to see him get really bad, so he hid it from you."

"Why tell me this shit now, then?"

"Because you need to know. You're carrying on just like your damn daddy."

I laughed at her when she said that. Getting up from the table, I knew my time coming over to Momma's house was over.

"You know what? You're just bitter like the rest of them."

She shook her head. "No, Son. I want you to see that if you keep going down this road, you may end up…"

"I'll never end up like that. I wrap up every time," I said, but she kept shaking her head. "I ain't no dumb motherfucka out here. I ain't getting that shit."

"Son, watch your mouth!"

She had me fucked up, thinking I would get that shit, but she didn't stop with that. "There is more than one way to die, you hear me?"

I heard her loud and clear, but none of those ways were going to involve me.

"Look, Momma. I love you, but I gotta get to work." I grabbed my keys and headed for the door.

"Son, you listen to me. Change your ways before it's too late."

I nodded and gave her a kiss on the cheek.

"No hard feelings, Momma, and I don't mean to be disrespectful, but I'm good, okay? I know what I'm doing." I left her with that, leaving out the back door to my car.

"Pops never had bitches like this on his team," I told myself as I walked to my BMW. Kiara hadn't asked for it back, and I had no intention of giving it up.

I got inside and started the engine, listening to it purr. I knew my Momma was just talking shit. Wasn't no way I was getting AIDS. Niggas only got killed from pussy when they were stupid, and I was far from that.

I had Arianne in my corner, and a new bad bitch

eating out of my hand. I had all of this shit under control and wasn't shit going wrong, because I was a better man than my Pops. He never had a business like my shop. I was gonna make it rich off my barbershop and show Momma her son wasn't no bum ass nigga. I was somebody and I wasn't going anywhere.

14

Ariane

Dick hardness makes a man blind; especially when they are so ready to fuck that they don't inspect anything—not even the condom. So it wasn't hard to poke small holes in the gold packaging of DeWayne's condoms for weeks. Now I was at the shop, locked in the bathroom about to check to see if I was pregnant.

For the last few days, I had a slight fluttering in my stomach on the right side, and I just knew that it was a baby growing in there. I fished around in my purse for the pregnancy test I kept in there, waiting for the right moment to take it. Just so happens that the right moment is this morning right before my first client.

I bought the test weeks ago when I first came up with this plan and hid it in my purse so DeWayne wouldn't find it. And now, after all this time, I was taking the test that was going to change my life with the man I loved.

Sitting down to pee on the stick, I closed my eyes and prayed for what I already knew to be true. "Dear Lord, give me a second chance at being a mother. What I couldn't be to Avianna, please, Lord, let me be for this baby. Amen."

Before I could even get the cap back over the pregnancy test, I could already see the two lines forming. One line for no and two lines for yes.

"Thank you, Lord," was the first thing that came to my mind, but the second was Ms. Lawyer Bitch.

He hadn't mentioned her name since he came to my house that night, and I kept my pussy and my lips wrapped tightly around his dick so he didn't have much time to think about anybody else. With his mom being sick and him having to spend more time with her, he didn't have time for anything but me and the shop, and now we were going to have an addition to our new family.

Coming out of the bathroom, I couldn't hide the smile on my face. But looking at the deep frown on DeWayne's face, I thought about maybe telling him another time. He'd had an attitude all morning, since he came into the shop. Looking down at the pregnancy test in my hand, I knew I couldn't wait until later. I had to tell him now.

"Babe, can I talk to you in the supply room?" I asked him as he got done with a customer.

"Can we talk later? I got people."

"No... We need to talk now, please. I have something to tell you."

"Aight, man. This better be important."

I followed him into the stockroom and let it go. Handing him the pregnancy test, I said the words I'd been rehearsing in my head for weeks.

"Baby, I'm pregnant."

I put the test in his hands, smiling like a nigga that just got taken off child support.

"What the fuck you mean, you're pregnant?"

DeWayne looked so fine with his barber cape on.

Usually, I would have fucked him right here in the supply room between the relaxer and shampoo shelves, but right now, he didn't seem happy like I thought.

What I thought was going to be laughing, crying, and a happy face was turning into a fucking nightmare.

"Just what I said, DeWayne. I'm having your baby."

He shook his head so hard I thought it was going to fall off his body. I wasn't sure if that meant he didn't want a baby or that he didn't want another baby with me. *Would he be acting this way if that bitch was pregnant?*

"Hell no... I strap up every time."

I had to cover my mouth to keep from smiling. Yeah, he wrapped up but, maybe if his lazy ass would go buy the condoms himself, I wouldn't have had the time to punch holes in them.

"Well baby, slipups do happen." I didn't feel like taking him through the birds and the bees talk. "I mean, aren't you going to give me a hug or something?" I tried touching him, but he pushed me away.

"I don't have no time for no babies. I'm up to my ass in bills, and now you come in here with this shit." He closed his eyes and rubbed his temples like a severe headache was bouncing through his brain.

I laughed at him. "But baby, we got money. I'm making money, you're making money... I mean…"

"Bitch, that's not enough!"

I stopped talking; he had never called me that before.

"You think that little bullshit you make braiding hair is going to pay for my kids, take care of this shop, and take care of us?" He was screaming now, so close that I felt his breath on my face.

"Why are you screaming at me and calling me a bitch?"

His face softened when I asked him.

"Look, I'm sorry, but I can't have no kids right now. I got too much shit going on." He rubbed his head so hard, I thought this skin was going to come off.

"We'll figure something out. I can call up some people and get some of the new clothes sold."

"Then what? Next month, keep calling them same niggas? I got bigger dreams than that."

"What could be bigger than this shop and us starting a family?" I screamed at him, and he started laughing.

"Are you crazy? We might be rich to these ghetto motherfuckas, but I'm trying to be wealthy."

I hadn't heard him say that before, and I didn't even understand the fucking difference. To me this was better than sleeping in a jail cell or selling dope and watching my back.

He pulled me close to him, rubbing my head. For the first time since telling him I was pregnant, I felt like he was showing me some kind of compassion.

"Look, you gotta get an abortion."

My heart stopped. "A what?"

Before he could answer, the room went dark.

"What the fuck?" DeWayne opened the supply room door, and the shop was dark, too.

"Yo, DeWayne, it's an electric company truck out here," Trae, another barber, screamed to the back.

DeWayne ran to the front of the shop and out the door as I walked out and watched from the window. My client would be here soon, but watching DeWayne argue with the electric man, I felt sick again. Not like I was going to throw up, but like I was sick in the head. This nigga didn't have no money for real, and now that Ms. Lawyer bitch was out of the picture, it seemed like all the shit that I didn't know about him was coming out.

"He better get Kiara's ass back, or we gonna be

looking for a new shop," one of the stylists said from behind me, which instantly sent me into go mode.

I spun around and faced the bitch that said it. "He don't need that bitch, Kiara! She ain't the only one that has money."

Before they could talk, DeWayne was back through the door. "Aight, everybody. We got a small issue with the electric and a mistake on the billing. I'm going to have to close down today, but we will be back open tomorrow."

"Boo, I can take care of it."

DeWayne was already at his station taking off his apron and grabbing a hat. "Naw, I gotta go. Make sure you make an appointment to take care of what we talked about." He looked down toward my stomach, talking about the abortion that I wasn't going to have. "And lock up the shop. I'll call you later."

And then, jumping into the car that the lawyer bitch bought him and burning rubber off the lot, he was gone.

I wondered how many heads I would have to braid to get the money that bitch got. Money was the only thing that DeWayne wanted, and the only move I had left to win his heart.

15

Kiara

It took a while, but I was finally having days where I didn't cry myself to sleep. This morning I woke up refreshed, because today my first day in my new office. I'm packing boxes and putting away picture frames and books. On none of these pictures was DeWayne's face, and I was okay with that.

When I said it was over a month ago, on the night when I cried myself to sleep, I said I was done. But now, looking down at my phone ringing and DeWayne's name popping up on the screen, I had a feeling some bullshit was about to happen.

"What, DeWayne?" I answered the phone, but I had no time for his bullshit this morning.

"You got the electric cut off?" he screamed through the phone.

I laughed at his dumbass. If he spent most of his time taking care of bills instead of chasing these hoes, the electric wouldn't be cut off.

"Good morning to you too, DeWayne," I laughed in his ear

"Man, this shit ain't funny. Why you playing games?"

And that made me laugh even harder. Looking at the view of the city from my office, I imagined that he was sitting in that shitty barbershop with the lights off wondering where he went wrong.

"Games, DeWayne? What games? I don't play games, remember? Did you not get the contract that I sent to you?"

"Yeah, I got that shit. So what?"

"If you would've read it, you'd have seen that I was no longer paying the utility bills at the shop. Also, I'm separating myself from any legal ramifications incurred by the shop."

"But you're my partner. How do you do that?"

Now this is getting hilarious. This motherfucker has lost his mind.

"I'm no longer your partner, DeWayne. In life or in this business."

"But you can just leave me like that? You're the one who fucked your boss!"

I remember that night like yesterday, but I still wasn't taking shit back. I made the right decision for me and for my future.

"If I counted how many bitches you've fucked, you would win hands down." He had at least 20 to my measly one. I was done pleading with him, and I was moving on.

"But the shop... You know that's my way to make money."

"Guess what, DeWayne. I don't give a fuck anymore." His begging was literally making me sick. As much as I wanted to keep laughing in his face, I had to get something to eat or drink to calm my rumbling belly before court. "DeWayne, I have to go."

"Can we sit and talk about this? Maybe later on, over

dinner?" That was him always trying to weasel his way back into my life.

My stomach was doing cartwheels, so I agreed just to get him off the phone. "Yeah, whatever. I gotta go."

Dropping the phone, I ran for my new private bathroom that was connected to my new office. As soon as I was inside, my stomach exploded, sending my breakfast up in chunks into the toilet.

"Ms. Lawrence, are you okay?"

My secretary was at the door, but I couldn't look at her. The vomit kept coming until I was left hanging over the toilet with nothing in my stomach. "Get me a water," I managed to say after it was all done. My secretary didn't have to walk far—the mini fridge in my office was stocked full of refreshments.

"Here you go." She handed me the water.

To think that on my first full day as partner, I was on my knees vomiting into the porcelain.

"I threw up just like that when I was pregnant," my secretary said.

I felt like someone kicked me in my back and stopped my lungs from working. "Pregnant? I'm not pregnant." I got to my feet, swished the water around my mouth, and spit it into the sink.

"Sure... Yes, ma'am. Ummm…"

She looked down at the papers in her hand, trying not to make eye contact with me, but it was too late. I took off my suit jacket and flung it to the floor. How dare she make an assumption that I'm pregnant?

"Call the cleaners and get my suits up here." We had a cleaner on the main floor specifically for executives, and I was thankful for it now that there were fresh vomit stains on my suit. Vomit on my clothes was not a good look for my first meeting of the day.

"Yes, ma'am. Right away."

Brenda scurried off, but I called after her. "See if you can get to a drug store and grab me a few tests." She smiled, but my frown quickly dissolved whatever happiness she was feeling. "And if you breathe a word, you won't be at this company any longer. Do we understand each other?" I didn't mean to be such a bitch, but this was serious.

"Yes, ma'am," she said and left, giving me a chance to think.

With how depressed I had been over the last month and wrapping up old cases in preparation for my new role, I had completely forgotten about my period. I always kept track on my desk calendar, but that was packed away in the half dozen boxes in my new office.

Please don't be pregnant. I turned sideways in the mirror and as soon as I did I felt it, a grumble in my stomach like last time. I already knew what to do—just lean over the toilet and let it all out.

16

DeWayne

Sitting in my car in the middle of the night, I kept trying to figure out how much an abortion would cost. It had been awhile since I paid for an abortion, so I didn't remember how much it would cost, but whatever the price, Ariane was going to get one. I wasn't going to be a daddy again, and kids or a new baby momma weren't in my plan of getting paid.

I told her we would talk about this situation later, but the talking would be me taking her to an abortion clinic in the morning.

Momma was right, I was eating like somebody was pregnant. But she wouldn't be that way for long.

The sound of my phone ringing filled the car. Seeing Ariane's name used to make my dick jump, but now I felt stupid and threw the phone down in my passenger seat. I wasn't in the mood to talk to her about it tonight, since I spent my day paying bills and trying to call Kiara. I begged her to kick me down some more money, but after a while she stopped answering my calls. The bills were always

Kiara's responsibility. I would just give her money, and she would take care of things.

Sometimes I didn't have to give a dime; she would just keep shit going while I stacked my money and paid off my baby mommas. That was a ride or die for you, but some shit I just can't overlook.

I should have known that eventually she was gonna stop taking care of shit, but between Ariane and my new squeeze, I've been preoccupied. You see, a down ass nigga like me, I gotta keep two in the bag and one in the hole. I always had a bitch on deck, and shit going bad with Kiara wasn't gonna stop my show.

I looked at the contract that Kiara was talking about, and she was right. It said that she wasn't paying any more bills and at the end of the month she was terminating her contract.

Figuring out a way around this always involved me going back to her, but how could I get the thought of someone else fucking Kiara out of my mind? Forgiving her for what she did wasn't an option. My Daddy always said, "Once a dirty bitch…," but with all the pussy I got over the years, how could I blame her for stepping out on me?

Shit was confusing, but all I knew was I had a major cash flow issue. Between the shop and everything else I had going on, I needed that bitch.

But tonight, I just needed to clear my head. I finally found somebody that I could be with who didn't demand shit from me, and I didn't want nothing from her. Sitting on the parking lot, tucked back in the corner, I waited for her.

Jena's not your average bitch. She has her own money, car, and crib. But most of all, she had something that attracted me to her even more—she had a man.

You see, I fucked up before because I was fucking with

bitches who were single. They would catch feelings for me and want me to be all theirs. But of course, I was tied down to Kiara, and who didn't want to be in her spot?

Being seen around town with me put a spotlight on her. We were always jumping out of fly cars, going on shopping sprees at the mall, and flying out on trips. Every bitch in town stalked Kiara's Facebook and IG accounts trying to figure out what we were doing, so they could throw a wrench in my game, but not this time.

Jena was smart and occupied, only able to see me at night when her man was at work, and all she wanted to do was fuck. No dates, no love letters, and not even much talking. I met her when she brought her son in for a haircut. Her fat ass squeezed inside some spandex tights with titties that poked out of her top. Lucky for me, Ariane wasn't at the shop that day, so I pounced on that bitch like a lion on a gazelle.

Tonight, we were supposed to chill. Looking out the window, I saw her car creeping across the movie theater parking lot. We decided to meet here in the back, way on the other side of town, so no one would notice us.

She parked a few rows over and walked to my car, getting in with a hat low on her head and an oversized coat covering her up.

"You really aren't taking any chances," I laughed at her when she was inside. I leaned over to give my baby a hug.

"You know we can't leave nothing to chance, living this life."

She laughed and so did I. I felt good finally dealing with someone who knew me and what I was going through. As much as I was trying to protect the people I cared about, so was she.

"Yo, wassup with you making all that damn noise this morning?" I grabbed her thigh as she pulled off her coat.

"Sorry, baby. I'll make it up to you. I had to leave; your friend was acting a fool."

I saw those same plump titties that I loved to suck were pressed down in a spandex tank top with some tights covering up everything below. But I had to comment on what she said.

"What you mean, 'my friend'? That nigga ain't my friend." I wouldn't be fucking my friend's girl. Rick was just a nigga I knew from around the way, and if his hoe was willing to fuck me, then who was I to turn her away? Plus, he was always bragging about how her pussy was the wettest in town, so I couldn't help but give it a try.

"Well he was calling and acting crazy so I had to go." She was singing me a sob story, but that shit was the last thing I wanted to talk about. We came here to fuck, not talk about our personal lives.

"So, how are we gonna do this? My backseat isn't that big." That was what I missed most about my truck. I can't count how many bitches I had back there when I pushed back the third row. But now, in this BMW, the leather seats felt great but the room to smash was held to a minimum.

"Actually, I was thinking that we could try something different." She licked her lips as she pulled off her hat.

"Like what?"

"Just drive," she told me, turning up the radio.

Putting the car into drive, I crept out of the parking lot and into the night. We were gliding down the streets for a while when my passenger made her move.

Angling over the armrest, I knew instantly what she was about to do, and my dick swelled in my pants at the thought. This was the shit that Kiara used to do, and the things that Ariane refused to do. She talked all that shit about wanting to be better than Kiara, but that bitch wasn't as thorough as Kiara. At the same time, Kiara didn't have the dirty hustle that Ariane did. But Jena didn't nag the way the other two did, so it was like a switch.

"Lean back and enjoy baby," she told me, and with one hand on the steering wheel, I did just that. My zipper came down and my dick flopped out as the music played and some bass-filled song sent the speakers knocking. Shit like this was what relaxed me—a little bit of danger on some voyeur shit while being with a bitch who didn't nag me.

"Damn, girl." She was like a tight Jacuzzi, covering my dick in her hot mouth and sucking it while I drove. This shit required an intense amount of concentration, but my only instinct was to pull over.

"Drive faster, baby," she said over the bass in my car and with her mouth full of my dick.

I did as she said, my leg trembling with every twirl of her tongue, but I still pressed down on the gas.

"Shit, girl." I grabbed a fist full of her hair with my other hand and tried to keep cool as she sped up, licking faster, taking me deeper inside her jaws.

I could feel my dick about to explode as I breezed down the road. A honking horn made me jump. I grabbed the wheel and tried pulling the car over, but I was too late. Jena jumped up, screaming just as I looked up to see the truck coming straight for us.

17

Ariane

"Hoe... Homewrecker... Side bitch..."

I heard whispering as I walked into church, but every time I looked around, I didn't see anyone. Just smiling faces looking forward in the sanctuary and clapping their hands to the music as if they didn't even notice me.

I've been thinking about going to have my soul blessed lately. Nothing with DeWayne has been right, and I have so much wearing on me. Now, in this church, I just wanted to bring all my sins to God and lay them down.

I hadn't been to church in so long that I barely remembered the words to the Lord 's Prayer. In prison, we had small little group churches, but in there, I only prayed for the Lord to turn me into a bird so I could be free.

Now, as I look to the front of the church, the whole sanctuary is filled with faces I don't recognize, and like a group of soldiers trained for precision, they all turned to look at me at the same time. They all went from smiling to frowning as they stared at me. I want to ask what they are looking at, but their screams drown out my voice.

"Hoe... Homewrecker... Side bitch..."

The whispers were now screams. I couldn't be in church; I had to be in hell with demons the way these people were yelling at me. Everyone was chanting like we were at some kind of football game, calling me every name in the book. I want to leave, but my feet are glued to the floor. The music shifts from a church hymn with a piano to an organ that quiets the screams and name calling. Everyone goes quiet and back to smiling like nothing happened.

I recognize the tune immediately. "Here Comes the Bride" fills the room, and that's when I realize I'm not at a normal Sunday church service, I'm at a wedding. But whose wedding?

We all stand, facing the back of the church, and I see her running down the aisle, a white dress with a veil, a silver knife in her hand.

"You bitch, stay away from my husband!"

It's her, alright. Ms. Lawyer Bitch in the flesh. Before I can put my hand up to block the knife, a loud buzzing invades my mind, ripping me from the dream.

Shooting straight up in the bed, I realize I'm no longer in the church but in my bedroom.

"Shit!" Turning to my side, I wanted to tell DeWayne all about it, then laugh and hold him. But he wasn't there, and he hadn't been there all night from what I could tell. I hadn't seen him since earlier at the shop. I had called his phone a dozen times but no answer.

"That bitch wishes she had a husband." I hated those type of dreams, the ones where you can't move or say anything, because in real life, I would have whooped that bitch's ass all around that church. "He will never be your husband," I told the room, as if Ms. Lawyer Bitch was standing right in front of me.

Instead, I was alone in the darkness, searching for my cell phone.

It was official, I was pregnant. I knew my body like the back of my hand—that probably came from my prison days when there was nothing for me to do but get in tune with myself. I took the test earlier just to show DeWayne, but I already knew there was something growing inside me.

The baby was only as big as a golf ball, or maybe even smaller right now, but I could swear I felt her.

My phone rang again, and I found it between my bed and the wall. It was DeWayne, and my smile couldn't be erased. I wanted him home to be with me, but when I answered, all I heard were sirens.

"Hello."

"Yes. Your name is saved as 'wife' on this phone. I just found it at a car accident and the ambulance just left. I'm trying to get it back to its owner. I saw the whole thing."

I looked at the phone again to make sure I wasn't tripping. "What are you talking about?" This made no sense. What accident was this motherfucka talking about?

"This phone belongs to someone who was just in an accident. A black BMW."

I screamed so loud, I thought I scared the person who called.

"Yes...my husband." All I could think was that DeWayne was dead. "Where are they taking him?" I asked, already jumping up to get my clothes on.

"Mercy General. I got his phone if you need it."

I didn't give a fuck about the phone. "Umm... I gotta go see about my husband."

"Okay. I work at the store on 15th and Taylor. Just come in and ask for Joey. I'll have it for you."

"I'll call you back." I hung up, grabbed my shit, and

headed out the door, not caring about that damn phone. "Baby, please be okay." Tears stung my eyes, but I had to go be by my man's side. This was no time for me to cry.

18

Kiara

I drove to the hospital with my heart beating just as fast as the car was moving.

"Please, Lord. Please." I begged for DeWayne's life as I parked and ran into the emergency room.

"I'm here to see DeWayne Coleman. He was in a car accident." My hair was wrapped and I was in sweats, but when I got the call, there was no time for me to wake up and beautify myself. All I knew was the navigation company alerted me of an accident. After calling the police station to confirm, I got the name of the hospital where DeWayne was being taken.

"Down the hall, room 8," the attendant told me, pressing a button to get me behind the double security doors.

I felt like I was in a movie, looking from room to room until I found my love bandaged in a neck brace and strapped to a bed.

My entire first day as a fully functioning partner had been spent in chaos, and now it was even worse. The man

I loved, or was trying not to love, was hurt. That meant the father of my child was in danger.

After getting my head out of the toilet, I managed to go to a meeting, but all day I couldn't help but think about my stomach. I couldn't sleep all night. At first, I thought it was about what the doctor told me at my emergency appointment earlier that day. The prescription for prenatal pills and all the do's and don'ts of pregnancy were confusing, so I thought maybe I was simply nervous about that. But once I got the call telling me my car had been involved in an accident, my heart slid to the floor.

DeWayne was in bad shape. The police officer who told me where he was said the car had twisted metal, which probably meant that it was totaled. I was surprised I was even able to make it here with how nervous and scared I was. I was surprised I didn't have a damn wreck.

"DeWayne. Baby. Oh, baby. Oh my God." I had never seen him like this. He looked so helpless laying on the hospital gurney.

"Kiara." He tried reaching for me, but there wasn't much he could do from the hospital gurney with his neck in a brace.

"Baby, what happened?" I asked.

He tried explaining that he was driving and must have fallen asleep.

"DeWayne, didn't I used to tell you that you need to get some damn rest? What if you died? What would happen to me and the baby?" I couldn't believe I said that, but seeing him like this pulled on my heart strings. I was overcome by emotion, and tears fell.

"What baby?"

Now I had to explain what I said. I tried figuring out a good way to word this. Maybe I could tell him I meant his youngest daughter. "I was just speaking of all of the kids. What do I tell them?"

But he gave me a weird look, even with a neck brace

"No... Baby, are you?" He tried sitting up but winced in pain.

"Be still. What did the doctors say?"

"Damn the doctors! Are you pregnant?"

I never thought I could get pregnant. I told him a million times that I couldn't, but sure as shit, here I was, standing in front of him positively pregnant with his child. I never wanted to tell him like this. I planned on calling him over or taking him to dinner, not saying something this important in a hospital emergency room with unknown people walking around, voices over the P.A system, and beeping machines interrupting us. But looking at DeWayne, seeing him so close to being taken away from me, everything that pissed me off about him evaporated away. I just wanted to love him, beg him to come back home, raise this baby together, and pretend like the bullshit between us never happened.

I only smiled, and before he could answer, a man in a white doctor's coat walked in.

"Well, Mr. Coleman, we can take this brace off. It looks like you have no fractures, just a concussion." A nurse wasn't far behind, taking the brace off DeWayne and helping him up.

"Just take it easy and get some rest. Visit your primary care physician and...

"DeWayne... DEWAYNE..."

I heard a voice calling his name, and a few seconds later, there she was.

"Oh my God, baby, I..." She looked from him to me and then back again. "What is that bitch doing here?"

"Bitch, who you callin a bitch?"

"You know who I'm talking to, bitch. I'm his woman now. I'm the one carrying his baby."

DeWayne shook his head.

"You're not pregnant, you lousy ass bitch, and I want you out of here! I am having a family discussion with my man."

"Your man? He's my man!"

"No, bitch. You are the side bitch, and you need to get in your place." I looked at DeWayne, waiting for him to check this bitch.

"Arianne... Maybe you should go. I'll talk to you later."

Her face dropped to the floor. "Oh, so you get in an accident, and I come up here to see about you and you push me away? Are you going to act like this when I have your baby?"

I laughed at the bitch. This was the oldest trick in the book.

"What the fuck are you laughing at?"

"Ladies, we need you both to leave," the nurse interjected, but I wasn't going anywhere.

"I'm laughing at you, hoe. You're no more pregnant than a tranny on gay pride day! But me, on the other hand, I'm pregnant for real. By this man." I pointed at DeWayne and her eyes were as big as apples. "Now carry on and get the fuck out." I pushed her toward the door. I was tired of this bitch. Every time I tried to talk to DeWayne, she was around.

"Don't touch me, bitch. I'm pregnant!"

The words stopped me from moving, but I laughed so hard I thought I was going to throw up again.

"Pregnant? Bitch, please. I'm the one who's pregnant, and yes, I'm keeping it." I stepped to this tired hoe once and for all.

"Ladies, we need you to please take this outside. Please calm down."

I heard the doctor talking, but I wasn't paying attention. The emergency room was buzzing, but I saw nothing but this bitch. DeWayne called my name and stood up, trying to pull me away, but I was done with this. Fire burned inside me, and it jumped from my heart down into my fist. As quickly as the thought came, I jumped from where I stood and punched that bitch in the face.

It was as if the world stopped moving when my fist collided with her face. "Yeah, bitch! You wanna steal somebodies man?" I yelled at her, then hit her as quick as I could before they broke us up and pulled her away.

"Kiara, quit that shit!" DeWayne held me back, but I wasn't done.

"Fuck that! You get rid of that bitch and marry me, or I'm done." I said the words and I meant it. "I'm not fucking playing, DeWayne. I'm done with this shit."

I didn't care if he almost died in an accident. I was done going back and forth with this shit. Grabbing my purse, I walked out and saw the bitch screaming with a few security guards around her. DeWayne walked out with me, his arm draped over my shoulder. "You can't be out here fighting. What if you get reported to the Bar Association?"

"I don't give a fuck about that." He was right but at the moment I didn't care about getting in trouble. Bitches like her made me sick. Shaking his head at me and smiling.

"What…its your fault this shit is going on." I told him.

"Baby, I'll do it. You hear me? I'll do it. Let's get married!" As he grabbed me and hugged me, I looked over his shoulder. Seeing that bitch frowning and damn near having a heart attack as she went crazy made my fucking year.

She tried to break up my family and take my man, but if I knew anything, I knew DeWayne. He would stray, but at the end he would always come back to me, and now was no different.

Chapter 19

He waited for his wife in the living room. What was usually a one hour yoga class had now turned into four hours with no call, text, or voicemail of her whereabouts.

He went from being mad, to pissed, to a full rage. As the hours passed, he thought maybe something had happened to the woman he loved. Finally, he saw the headlights of her car deep in the driveway.

Minutes passed before he heard keys at the door. Instead of swinging the door open to ask her where she had been, he sat in the dark, still like a snake waiting for the right time to strike.

Coming through front door as quiet as a mouse, Jena tried to make as little sound as possible. As she walked slowly toward the stairs, a flick of the living room lamp made her jump.

"Where the fuck have you been?" Rick demanded, his baritone voice booming through the room.

"I... I was in an accident." Her voice shook.

"An accident?" He grabbed the blinds and looked out at her car. "I don't see shit wrong with your car."

"Not my car. I was with a friend." She hated the words as soon as they came from her mouth. Saying "a friend" sounded too much like male friend and that was strictly forbidden in her marriage, an offense that would get her slapped or worse.

"A friend? What friend? You were supposed to be at yoga." His questioning put him in detective mode, sending him up from the couch, and moving toward his wife.

"A friend from yoga. We went to get yogurt after class and we got in an accident."

He looked down to see a hospital bracelet on her arm and started to believe her story, but there were holes that needed to be filled. "Why didn't you call and tell me?"

Her shaky hands pulled out a busted up cell phone. "I broke my phone in the accident, plus you were here with the baby. Thought I would just explain when I got home."

Rick wasn't sure of all this. His mind was moving, but everything he asked, she an answer for. "Well, who did the report? Was it your *friend's* fault?" he asked.

Jena shook her head no. "Some car came in and side swiped us."

He looked her up and down, not sure how to feel as he watched her grimace in pain.

"Are you hurt?"

"Just whiplash."

Rick nodded, keeping eye contact with his wife. Something didn't seem right, but he couldn't put a finger on it. Instead he grabbed her jacket and pulled her close. "You get into something like that you call me. I could have called one of the guys from the force to come check on you."

His badge and tenure on the police force were good for something.

"Yes, baby. I understand. I just...didn't want you to worry." She patted his fist until he loosened his grip on her shirt. *Please, Lord, not tonight.* Smiling, she prayed that he wouldn't be upset and that he bought her story.

"Well, junior is asleep," Rick said, looking over his wife's curves. Tonight was usually the only night they spent together, but instead, he had spent his evening on the couch, pissed off and ready to fight. Now, he wanted way more than an argument.

"Yeah, I figured that. I'm gonna go take a shower and lay down. I'm pretty sore." Jena tried taking a step up the stairs, but Rick took another pull at her jacket.

"Sleep... Why sleep when you can have this?" He pulled her hand down to his hardened dick poking out of his slacks. "Did I tell you I solved a case today?"

She smiled, patting him on the chest. "Nope. Congrats, babe! But tonight…"

He cut her off, not taking any objections tonight. "Go ahead upstairs and get cleaned up and ready for me."

He disregarded everything she said. The fact that she was in an accident, her soreness, and especially the fact that it was the middle of the night. Nothing mattered to Rick but whatever he wanted.

"Ummm, baby can we…"

"What? You don't want to please your husband? If you don't want to please me, then who are you pleasing?" He pushed her to the wall, her back hitting the drywall with a thud.

"Nobody, baby. I'm just tired and sore from the accident and…"

"Go upstairs and put on that one thing I like." He ignored everything she said as he pulled handcuffs from his waistband. "And tonight, we are going to play detective and suspect."

She mustered up a smile just for her husband. The

penalty for not complying would be way worse than the few minutes of cooperation. "Okay, baby. Just for you."

She started up the stairs as he sent a hard slap to her ass. She grimaced in pain from the hit, but she kept going.

Rick watched Jena disappear up the staircase and soon heard the bathroom door close and the shower begin. That's when he went to work, grabbing his cell phone and dialing the police station.

"Fifth precinct."

Rick recognized the voice immediately. "Hey, Donnie. It's B man. Slow night?"

"Haha! You should be asleep man. Yeah, it's crazy slow tonight. Of course, it would be when you're off. No murders."

Rick laughed. "Hey, I got a question. Can you see if there were any accidents near 37th and Park?"

Rick heard a few strokes of a keyboard and a grumble from Donnie. "Nope, nothing that I see."

His eyes shifted upstairs.

"Why, something you working on?"

"Naw, just trying to see about an accident my wife's friend was in."

"Oh... Well, you could wait a day or two and search the report system. It will all be in there by then," Donnie reported.

"Cool. I'll see ya tomorrow." With that Rick hung up, his detective mind going over the details that his wife gave and filing them in his memory bank as he scaled the stairs. *This bitch better not be lying,* he thought to himself as he slowly opened the bathroom door and watched her lather up in the shower.

Rick prided himself on a running a household with military precision, and all of that began with his wife. If she didn't disclose her whereabouts for every second, that only meant one thing in his eyes. He flexed his fist, then slowly closed the bathroom door and walked to their bedroom.

I said I wouldn't hit her again, he told himself, practicing the breathing techniques that the counselor taught him in their marriage counseling class.

"One…Two….Three…" He counted and breathed deep as he unbuttoned his shirt.

He hoped she wouldn't make him break his promise, but lying was an offense he could only deal with by using his fists. *I don't give a shit what I said. If she's lying, I'm gonna fuck her up,* he thought as he peeled his shirt off and placed his police department issued revolver on the night stand. But as the shower went off and he got comfortable in bed, he convinced himself to believe his wife.

After that last slapping around, she's done doing wrong, he told himself as Jena, with the towel wrapped loosely around her damp skin, stepped into the room and softly closed the door behind her.

"You ready to question me, detective?" she asked as she let the towel fall to the floor. "Because I want to tell you everything I know."

Her breasts were perky and ready to be devoured, but little did Rick know that his wife no longer saw his burly frame but that of a sleeker, more built man. The same man whose dick she had been sucking so well tonight that it had caused an accident. That was the man she would be making love to, not her husband. Her fantasy was the only thing that kept her sane in a marriage full of chaos.

Rick told himself that he loved her, and Jena told herself that she had to stay with a man who abused her. They both were telling themselves lies, yet no one was brave enough to tell the truth.

20

DeWayne

Blurting it out was the only way I could think to do it. With the sun creeping through the window, I had never been so sure of anything in my life.

"Kiara, will you marry me?" I thought about it all night, and this was the only thing I could do. She could barely rub the sleep out of her eyes before I asked.

I stayed up all night at Kiara's house. Way after she went to sleep, I prayed for the first time in years and thanked God for saving my life.

I went back to the last thing I could remember, which was Jena sucking me up and then the lights from the other car and the sounds of metal crashing and crumbling. The shit made it impossible for me to close my eyes and that meant I was doing a lot of thinking.

I could have been dead, and it was all over a bitch and getting my dick sucked. I was gonna take this shit to my grave, and now I was going to make the right decision.

"I was just talking last night, DeWayne." She sat up looking at me. "I wasn't really serious about us getting married. Just because I'm pregnant, you don't have to marry me."

I knew I didn't have to, but I wanted to. I felt it was the right thing to do. "I want to. I know I don't have to but... I'm tired of all this bullshit." That was the truth. I had clothes all over the city, from Ariane's to my Mom's and a few places in between. I just wanted one home and a place to lay my head.

"What about...everything at my job?"

I squeezed her hand, thinking about the night that I found out about what she did. "That shit hurt me, Keke. I can't even lie." I stretched my neck, the soreness getting worse as the hours went on.

"Yeah, you hurt me too."

I nodded hearing that. We had both hurt each other, and there was no way of turning back the hands of time on that.

"Let's just forget that shit. Let's start over with this baby." I rubbed her stomach, nothing was there yet, but soon her flat tummy would be a belly full of my baby.

"I could have lost you last night. You gotta be more responsible, babe."

She was right, and nobody needed to know what really happened, especially not Kiara. The shit between her and Ariane at the hospital proved it. I had to get my shit together.

I waited for Kiara to wake up, and when she did, I was waiting down on the side of the bed on one knee. "I wanna do it, baby. I want to marry you. Let you have that big wedding we always talked about." Maybe I was thinking about the shop and how I needed some help if I was bringing another shorty in the world.

"But what about that bitch being pregnant?"

I thought about Ariane for a brief second, thought

about Keke punching that bitch so hard that I felt it. "I'm not worried about her." I wasn't, but she probably wasn't going to get an abortion anymore. That was the shit we went through sometimes in life, but that's if her baby was even mine. Shit, I didn't know if this baby Kiara was having was mine either.

Shit was fucked up, but she was gonna get a nigga back on his feet. Especially now that I didn't have a car anymore. The truth was, I needed Kiara. So why not make her my wife?

"She is just trying to trap me, Kiara. I was blinded, baby, but I want you. I've only wanted you. I just…I've been tripping." I squeezed a tear out of my eye to show her that I was for real.

"Yes, I'll marry you!"

She was crying in my arms, but then she pushed me away, her eyes big as she fought to make it to her feet.

"What… What's wrong?"

She didn't answer as she ran out of the bedroom.

Seconds later, I heard the noises of a woman with morning sickness. It's official, I'm gonna be a daddy again.

I waited a few minutes, until I heard the toilet flush and the faucet come on.

This would be my life for a while, but it felt good to be back with Kiara. This was the only chick's house that I would call my home.

"Baby, you okay?" I called after her from the bedroom, already planning out the next nine months of my life.

Kiara was gonna want to have a big wedding. I already knew that. I laughed, thinking about me in a tux and her in a dress with a big baby underneath. She didn't say anything, but returned with a smile.

"I'll marry you under two conditions," she said, smiling with her robe wrapped around her.

"Anything, baby."

"One, that we get married today."

I swallowed hard. "Today? How is that even possible?"

"We can get our marriage licenses and have one of the judges in district 6 do it. I know one that owes me a favor."

I felt my head pound as she said that, but what choice did I have? "Okay... Why not? If you want today, Queen, then you got it." My Momma would probably pass out when I called to tell her, but she loved Kiara and always said she was the one I should pick. Now she was going to get her wish. "What's the other thing?" I asked her, now feeling tired and my body starting to ache even more from the whip lash.

"I want you to fire that bitch."

My eyes opened up wide. "What bitch?" I played stupid, but the look that Kiara gave me told me that she wasn't playing. "Okay. She's gone. It's just me and you." I pulled her close and hugged her.

"And I want all the other bitches gone, too, DeWayne."

This girl really did know me. "Baby, it's just me and you."

"I mean it, DeWayne. I know you can't be faithful, but marriage is something different," she said.

I agreed with her. "Kiara, it's just me and you baby," I said, but my mind drifted to Jena.

I wanted to call her, but I lost my phone in the accident. They took her to a different hospital, so I didn't know what the fuck was going on with her. Plus, we made a vow that we would only have minimum contact. She was just a bitch I was fucking, not my woman. I knew she wasn't dead, and that's all that mattered.

"Yeah, boo, I promise. Just me and you." I was aching bad now, my back hurting as she squeezed me. "Not too hard, boo. I'm still fucked up. I gotta go see about the car and get a new phone."

"Don't worry about all that, Mr. Coleman. Mrs. Coleman will take care of that." She laughed and pulled me into the bathroom. "You take a hot shower to loosen your muscles. I'm gonna call the insurance company and get the ball rolling to get you a new car."

I loved the shit out of this girl. There wasn't nobody like her. "Aight, boo. I love you, Mrs. Coleman." I peeled off my shirt as she turned the shower on for me.

"Okay baby. I love you." She gave me a kiss as I squeezed her ass, and then she was gone, leaving me alone in the bathroom.

This was the life, having a down ass bitch in my corner with enough bread to put a nigga back on his feet. I was still gonna be the same me, just a little bit smarter. If I would have known that all I had to do was marry her to make her happy, I would have done this shit years ago.

21

Ariane

Days after speaking to DeWayne at the hospital, I wondered why I even got involved with his dog ass in the first place. Now I was pregnant with his baby, and it obviously seemed like he didn't know what he wanted. So I was going to make it easy for him; I was going to leave his ass alone.

DeWayne didn't even have the decency to call and check up on me. I expected him to call and apologize the first day. But now that it was the third day with not one peep from that nigga, I was ready to start a war, but the more rational side of me prevailed. Maybe he was gaming the lawyer bitch out of her money, and he didn't have his cell phone, so how was he supposed to call me?

I went and picked his phone up from the guy who found it, thinking I was being the good girlfriend or whatever I was, but when I went through the messages, I felt like the biggest fool in the world. Texts to so many girls, I lost count, and so many pictures of random pussies that I thought I was going to be sick. He probably had the phone cut off or who knows how many pictures and texts I would have seen.

Here I was thinking that this nigga was exclusive to me, and all this time he was fucking other bitches.

But the games were over now. I wasn't just some side bitch anymore, I was his soon-to-be baby momma, and he was gonna treat me with some motherfucking respect or I was going to make his life a living hell.

Now, I was sitting outside the shop waiting for him to show up. I hadn't been here in days, thinking that it was best that I just give the shop a break. But as I flipped through his phone, I started thinking that I should take a break indefinitely.

Going inside as other stylists showed up, I decided to pack my shit and get out. I couldn't be here with this nigga and see him with all those hoes. Whether he was with Ms. Lawyer Bitch or not, I should just separate myself from this shit until I have the baby.

All eyes were on me when I went inside.

"Wassup, everybody!"

People looked sad as they stared, like someone had died. I hadn't been to the shop in days, but I didn't think it was that big of a deal. "What the hell is wrong with y'all?"

No one said anything. Some of them shook their heads, while some laughed and whispered to each other. The same old shop gossip bullshit. They probably heard that me and the Lawyer Bitch got into a fight the other night, but I didn't give a fuck.

Getting to my station, I started unplugging things and grabbing my products. It was time for me to go somewhere else.

"CONGRATULATIONS!"

A loud roar of cheering from everybody made me turn around, only to see DeWayne walking through the door like nothing was wrong. I wasn't sure what they were congratulating him on. The dudes gave him dap and the women gave him hugs. Looking out toward the parking lot, I saw a sparkling new BMW, so I could only guess what it was.

"Yeah, why you didn't invite me to the wedding?" I heard one of the barbers say, but I couldn't have heard right.

"Wedding... what wedding?" I looked down and instantly saw it, a sparkling white diamond ring on his left ring finger. "What the fuck!" I screamed in front of everybody from the customers to the stylists and barbers. I couldn't hold it in.

"What the fuck is that on your hand, huh?" I walked over to him, but he stopped me and grabbed my arm.

"Yo, I need to talk to you in the back."

I wasn't going into no back room to talk to him about this shit. I was discussing it right here in the open. "No, when were you going to tell me that you were getting married? When I was sucking your dick in the back room or when you were eating my pussy?" The barber shop erupted into laughter. "Did he tell y'all that he eats ass? Huh?"

"Yo, get the fuck out!" He pointed to the door, but I was already going.

"It's cool, motherfucka. I'll go," I said, grabbing my supplies. "But remember this. You and that bitch are going to be paying me child support."

More laughter erupted.

"Bitch, you ain't pregnant. I strapped up with you every time. You just a sack chaser. You better be lucky I came down your throat bitch." Now people were laughing so hard they were rolling around on the floor. "Now get yo broke ass out of here!" I couldn't do shit but leave.

"Yeah, whatever motherfucka. You better come get your shit before I throw it in the trash!" I screamed to him, walking to my car with my box of supplies as tears welled in my eyes.

I was determined not to shed one tear at least until I got down the street. But once I pulled off the lot, the tears started to come. My baby daddy did me this same way, discarding me when he was done, but I did years in prison for his ass.

DeWayne's phone was in the center console. I pulled over and pulled up his text messages. Starting with the first name I saw, I sent all them hoes a message, just in case mister playa wanted to keep fucking around. "You are fucking a married man. Leave DeWayne Coleman alone." I texted every last one of those bitches them from my phone.

"You don't wanna fuck with me, then tell me your wife is going to stay around so I can't get my money, bitch!" I screamed to the inside of my car.

My tears dried up as I typed out the messages.

"Quit crying over this busta and get you some money." I told myself, looking in the rearview mirror. I knew better than to fuck with a dog ass nigga like DeWayne. but now I was going to get two things.

First, I was going to get paid, and second, I was going to get another chance at being a mother. That was priceless and worth every stupid ass tear that I cried over DeWayne's ass. Soon enough, he would be the one crying, him and his dumbass bride.

I drove home and had already gotten myself together by the time I pulled up in front of my house. "Just call all of your clients and have them come to the house," I told myself as I made a mental list of everything I needed to do. Getting out of the car, I felt a bit faint, but that was just morning sickness or maybe I needed to eat.

"Hey, Ariane!" my neighbor called down to me, waving, but the look on her face as she ran to me was like she had seen a ghost. "Are you okay?"

"Yeah, just had a bad day at work. Why?"

She finally made it to me but she was looking down.

"What's wrong?" I asked, following her eyes when I saw it. My pants were soaked in blood. "Oh, my God."

"Calm down. Are you pregnant?"

I nodded as I fell to the ground, shaking and not sure what to do.

"Stay calm, I'm gonna call 911. Just relax and breathe," Claire said, but all I could think of was him.

This was DeWayne's fault. I got all upset with him and exerted myself.

"Yes, can you come quick. I believe my neighbor is having a miscarriage."

I heard the words, but I couldn't believe that Claire was talking about me. I cried for real this time. I was such a fucking fool and now the joke was on me.

22

Kiara

After a week of marital bliss, I was back at work, and it felt like I was walking on air. Looking down at the diamond ring that DeWayne picked out for me made me melt every time I glanced down at my hand. I purchased it for myself, but he promised that he would pay me back, which was fine with me just as long as I was Mrs. Coleman at the end of the day.

I took a few days off to spend with my new husband and get my morning sickness together, but now I was back at work and better than ever. DeWayne said the bitch is gone from the shop, he has been coming home every night, and I feel better than ever.

Now, in my office, I was busy working when my secretary broke through the intercom. "Mrs. Coleman?"

I had already changed my name at work, and hearing someone say it wasn't getting old yet.

"Yes?"

"Your insurance agent is on line 1."

I had been waiting for this call. I needed to find out exactly what the damage was going to be for DeWayne's accident. I was fully insured, but I still wanted to make sure there weren't any additional costs that the insurance wouldn't cover.

"This is Kiara," I answered.

"Yes, ma'am. This is Tracy from Insure One about the accident reported on the 18th."

As if I had another accident out there somewhere. "Yes. What are the damages?" I hated small talk. Usually talking to my insurance agent resulted in me paying more money, so I wanted to cut through all of that.

"It looks like everything will be covered by your policy."

That was great news! We didn't need to spend anymore unnecessary money. "Okay, well, that is awesome! Thanks for calling me about that..." I was ready to get her off the phone when her tone changed.

"But we need to speak with Mr. Coleman."

"About what?"

"Well, it says here that there was another passenger..."

I laughed before the woman could finish her sentence. "Ma'am, you must have your cases mixed up. There was only one passenger and that was DeWayne Coleman." I was ready to hang up on her. My pregnancy hormones were already giving me a short temper, and I had no tolerance for dumb shit right now.

"No, ma'am. I have the correct file. The police report states that there were two passengers. A man named DeWayne Coleman and a woman by the name of Jena Robinson."

I shook my head, feeling my brain about to burst in my skull from a headache.

"Ma'am are you still there?" she asked, but I was far away, drowning in the pits of hell.

Just when I felt like we were over something, another

problem came up. "Yes, I'm still here. Let me have DeWayne get back with you."

"Okay, thank you, ma'am."

I could hear it in her voice, as if she knew that it was some bullshit, and I was being lied to. He begged me to marry him, saying that he wasn't lying and that he was telling me the truth. I hung up on the insurance bitch and called DeWayne.

"Hey, baby, wassup?"

"Who the fuck is Jena Robinson, DeWayne?" I didn't wait; I was tired of beating around the bush on shit.

"What…?"

"She was in the car with you the night you so called 'fell asleep' and wrecked the damn car," I reminded him as he was acting like he didn't know shit.

"Baby, I…"

"I will see you at home tonight, DeWayne, and you better figure out a good fucking answer when you do come home." I slammed the phone down on the receiver, wondering if I made the right decision.

I pressed the intercom for my secretary. "Can you bring me the case file on annulments?" I asked her, not waiting for a reply.

I needed to brush up, because if this motherfucka came home telling me some dumbass lie, I was going to be single again quicker than his head could tell me a lie.

23

Ariane

I lost the baby, but it still didn't seem real. I bled like stuck pig all the way to the hospital crying and begging God but he didn't answer my prayers. Tonight, sitting in the living room, my television was the only thing that lit up the room, and I even had that on mute. I didn't want to hear anything because I was waiting for the Lord to tell me why he took my baby. Leaving me with no man, no baby, and no damn hope.

The doctor said it happens to plenty of women, but why did it have to happen to me? I spent the last days crying and crying, and the only reason I didn't have my ass in the bed crying myself to sleep this evening was because DeWayne called and said he was coming over.

I knew it wouldn't be long before he came to his senses, but I didn't want the usual sex before. I wanted to share with him that the baby I thought I was having was now gone.

Knocks on the door got me moving, but my mind was still in a daze and seeing him sent me into tears as I opened the door.

"Yo, what's wrong with you? I been trying to call you for days," he said closing the door. I hugged him and, surprisingly, he didn't push me away. "What the hell is going on, Ariane?"

"I had a miscarriage." I said the words myself for the first time since I came home. I hadn't talked to anyone except my neighbor Claire who helped me that day, and we still didn't say much to each other.

"Oh my God. I'm sorry." He acted really concerned and helped me to the couch as I cried on his shoulder.

"I was so mad at you the other day when I left. I got home and there was blood everywhere."

He listened to me talk as I described it all, how Claire rode with me in the ambulance and I spent the night in the hospital.

"Damn, A... 'm so sorry."

I looked into his brown eyes, but what I couldn't keep my eyes away from was his ring.

"Why did you go do that?" I pointed at it, the sparkling ring that he was still wearing today.

"It was the right thing to do. I have been running away from the right thing for so long. To be honest, I shouldn't have ever started up with you."

His words pierced my heart like an arrow. It was like he shot me like some deer in a forest and didn't give a fuck.

"So, you are going to say that to me right now?" I asked him and he must have been able to tell that I was getting mad.

"Look, I'm not going to argue. I gotta get home, so I'm gonna grab my shit and go." He stood up and walked into my bedroom like he owned this motherfucka.

"Yeah, I think you should go. I shouldn't have let this shit start with you either."

He acted like he was doing me a favor by fucking me,

but I did one for him. Taking him away from that drab, boring ass bitch, I was trying to save his life.

I heard drawers opening and closing in my bedroom and got mad all over again. "And don't be in there slamming my motherfuking drawers!" I screamed to him, but I didn't hear him respond.

He stomped into the living room and I expected him to tell me to shut up or maybe he just grabbed a couple of his things, but instead, I saw something gold land on the coffee table.

"What the fuck is that?"

Looking at it, I saw instantly that it was a condom. "With the kids you got, you don't recognize that it's a condom?" I asked. He really was a fucking idiot.

"What's up with these holes in it?" He flicked a switch on the wall, sending blinding light into the room.

Clear as day on the coffee table was the condom with small holes poked into it. When his dick was hard the holes were nonexistent, but I guess now, since he was grabbing his shit, he had time to inspect things.

"That…"

"You was trying to trap me." He had already put my plan together before I was able to explain.

"No… I…"

"Yeah, you were. That was in the top drawer, and that's where you always keep the condoms." He shook his head, looking down at me like he was disgusted.

"No… I…"

This wasn't the way I wanted to spend my night. He was back in my bedroom, knocking shit around and in minutes he was back with a bag full of clothes.

"Don't call me and definitely don't bring yo ass back around my shop. You see this?" He made a fist and showed me the ring. "This means I belong to somebody else and I'm done with all this bullshit."

"Fuck you!" I screamed at him, ready to jump up and hit him.

"No, bitch. Fuck you. That's why you had a miscarriage. You crazy ass bitch."

I felt like he punched me in the stomach. I was mad enough to hurt him, and if I'd had a knife in my hand, I would have stabbed him.

"Get the fuck out!" I screamed, my heart beating a million beats per second as I jumped up from the couch. He was already out the door and walking down to his car.

My phone rang, stopping me from running outside after him. Plus, I was still weak. "Calm down... Being mad is what got you into this in the first place." I had to think about myself now. As I walked toward my cell phone, I didn't even bother to look at the screen. Tears came as I answered the phone, looking over the small holes in the condom. He was right that I shouldn't have done that, but no one deserved a miscarriage.

"Yeah," I answered the phone, wanting whoever this was to leave me alone before they even said a word.

"This is detective Robinson."

I stopped crying. I instantly got a scared feeling like I was going back to jail.

"What is this about?"

"This is about a text you sent to one of our suspect's phones."

I wasn't sure what he was talking about until he read the text back to me. It was one I sent to all of DeWayne's bitches.

"Yeah... That was something I sent out in anger about my boyfriend." Why this had anything to do with a detective didn't make any sense. "But what does that have to do with anything?"

"What is your boyfriend's name?" he asked.

But DeWayne wasn't my boyfriend anymore. After what he said to me in here, he wasn't even my fucking associate.

"His name is DeWayne Coleman, but he isn't my boyfriend."

"DeWayne, from Cutting Edge?" The man's voice changed.

"Who the hell is this?" I looked at the phone, but it was an unknown call. "Hello?"

"Motherfucka…"

It sounded like the man dropped the phone, but I heard him cursing and knocking things around in the background. I did the only thing I could do and hung up.

"That shit is Mrs. Coleman's problem now. Good fucking riddance." I threw my phone across the couch. I was done with DeWayne and for good this time.

Chapter 24

Tracking applications were usually used on his underground phone tapping investigations. They called it "phone mirroring," meaning Rick could see everything one of his suspects typed or received on their phones. That meant texts and emails were all available for him to use as evidence in court, but tonight the only court that he was holding was in his living room.

After reaching out to a number that sent a text to his wife's phone, Rick was fuming mad, but he waited calmly for Jena to get home. After all, she was the main culprit in this affair, and as far as he was concerned, he just wanted to hear her say the words. He waited, but instead of the lights being off tonight, he turned them all on. He wanted her to see him.

Like always, she slipped into the house at 6:00 sharp. That was the time he told her to be home. Usually she came in, fixed dinner for the family, and helped their son with his homework, but there would be none of that tonight.

"Hey, baby," Jena said, smiling as she came through the door.

Rick couldn't hold his composure. He flew across the room, grabbing his wife and pinning her to the wall.

"You didn't think I would find out did you?" he asked, putting all of his burly bodyweight on her.

She struggled to breathe right as he grabbed a fist full of her hair.

"Say it! You didn't think I was going to find out!"

He slammed the back of her head into the wall, and Jena immediately started crying and begging.

"Don't beg now, bitch!" his voice roared through the house as he grabbed her by her head and dragged her through the living room, kicking her in her side as he pulled at her.

Screaming the entire way, Jena tried finding a weapon, anything that would stop Rick from his manic episodes, but there was nothing in her grasp.

"Baby, I'm sorry," she begged, her only other weapon against him. "Whatever I did, I can fix it!"

This type of behavior from her husband could be from something as little as not properly dusting a window sill to her worst offense, but she thought he had no idea about that.

"You can't fix shit, you dirty bitch. Did you like it? Did you like when he fucked you?"

Her worst fear was confirmed and the punch to the face sent her head spinning.

"I bet it felt great, didn't it bitch?"

He punched her so many times that Jena blacked out.

"Yeah, you liked it, but guess what. I'm gonna make sure he feels my wrath, too." He let her half-conscious body lay on the floor.

Wheezing for breath, Jena prayed for her life,

wondering where her son was and if her husband was done with his full-out assault against her. She tried listening for his footsteps in the other room, then heard his voice get closer again.

"Yeah, you're gonna learn that I love you more than anyone. Even that punk motherfucka DeWayne."

Jena heard the cock of his gun, and her body began shaking uncontrollably as she heard his footsteps get farther away, then the opening and slamming of the front door.

Jena yelled out, but her swollen lips and muffled voice were no match for the roaring of the engine in Rick's truck outside. She tried scrambling to her feet, but dizzy and disoriented, she could barely stand.

"Help..." she squealed when she heard his car leave the driveway. Finding her cell phone in her purse a few feet away, Jena dialed 911.

"911, what's your emergency?"

"My hus...band..." She tried hard to get the words out, spitting out blood as she spoke. "He tried to ki...ll me. He...lp..." Jena cried, praying for help. Most of all, she wished she could call and warn DeWayne.

"Ma'am, are you safe?"

Jena couldn't answer. Her eyelids got heavy as the room spun.

The police sirens sounded in the distance, but it may have been too late to stop Rick Robinson from his warpath of destruction.

25

Kiara

I got home way after dark. I decided to ride around the city to clear my mind and decide if I really wanted to go through the same shit with DeWayne over and over again. We were married now, and to go through the same things that we did back when we were just dating was stupid.

But the closer I got to the house, the sicker I felt. I figured it was maybe some type of nausea from the baby, but it felt a lot worse, like my stomach was tied in a tight knot. When I pulled in, I didn't see DeWayne's car, so I called him before I even got out of the car.

"Hello."

"When are you coming home so we can talk?" I asked him as I got out of the car and grabbed my things.

"I'm on my way now, baby. I just needed to pick up a few things, but I'm coming to you now."

"Okay...whatever."

"You're not mad at me, are you?"

Out of the corner of my eye, I saw a man get out of a truck. I had never seen him before, but he stared right at me, a frown on his face.

"Well, hurry home. I need you here."

"Okay, I'm about five minutes away."

I walked fast to the door, the keys ready in my hand, but the man was walking right to me now.

"May I help you?" I asked him before he got too close.

"Yeah, where is DeWayne?"

"Who is that?" DeWayne asked through the phone.

I had no idea what to say. "Ummm..."

"My name is Detective Rick Robinson. Are you his wife?"

"Yes, I'm his wife."

I heard DeWayne screaming, "No!" through the phone just as I saw the detective pull up a gun. Dropping the phone, I felt like screaming, but my voice got lost in my throat.

"Pick that motherfucking phone up and tell that nigga to get here or yo ass is dead."

26

DeWayne

I heard everything and pressed the pedal to the floor, getting home in seconds. Rick was standing outside, his gun pointing right at Kiara.

"Hey, yo, Rick. Man, this is between me and you. Leave my wife out of this."

He laughed and turned around to face me. "Yeah, leave your wife out of it, just like you left mine out of it?"

I didn't have any words to say to him on that. "Yo, man…"

"Yo, what, nigga?" He lifted the gun toward me.

How he knew where the fuck we stayed at was beyond me until I saw the badge dangling from his waistband. "Yo, you a cop Rick?"

"Yeah, motherfucka. How you think I figured this shit out?" He laughed like a crazy man.

I looked from him to Keke. She was shaking like a leaf. "I don't know, man. But it's not what you think."

"Don't worry. Yo bitch Ariane told me it all." I saw the color drain out of Keke as he said her name. "Yeah, she told me everything. I thought it was a code, nigga. You don't fuck with nobody's woman."

I shook my head—I had no words. I knew the code and should have never fucked with Jena. Holding my hands up, I tried to find the words, but Rick stole any thoughts that I had as he started screaming.

"Talk, bitch! Did you have her calling your name?" He took a step to Keke. "I bet I could make your wife scream."

"No! Leave her alone."

"Or what you gone do, nigga?"

I couldn't take this shit. I heard my Daddy in my ear telling me to die like a man or live like a coward. "Like I said, leave her alone."

I couldn't let him go after my wife, especially after this shit that I created. I heard the police coming, but they sounded too far away.

"You call the police?" Rick laughed. "Nigga, I am the police."

"I didn't call nothing. I'm here with my hands up, remember?"

"Or did you call?"

He took another step toward Kiara, and I jumped for his gun, trying to wrestle it from his hands. We wrestled like two grizzly bears until I heard a pop that sounded like a fire cracker.

"I"ll make sure to tell ya bitch... What is her name? Ariane?"

I heard her name, but I couldn't have heard him correctly.

"Yeah, Ariane, you tell that bitch thanks for letting me know it was you."

Keke screamed, begging the man, but her screams were in vain. My body got weak as I looked down to see blood fill my white shirt. I dropped to the ground. The sirens sounded like they were on top of me, but I couldn't turn my head to look.

"Stay with me, DeWayne. Stay with me."

But I couldn't. It was time, I could feel it. "I love you," I told Kiara, the only words I could make out before I faded away.

27

Kiara

At the hospital, I sat near the bed with his cold lifeless body.

It was over. All of the years of arguing and chasing each other ended in only a few minutes. His mother, Ms. Coleman, was the only other person in the room with me. Her screams echoed off the walls as she cried over her son, repeating the same words.

"I told you, son... I told you."

She cried and cried, but I was numb. I wonder what she had told him that I hadn't, how I begged him to stop doing the things he did. All of my tears had been cried years ago, begging DeWayne to be faithful to me. Tonight, all those things we fought about came to light.

"He told me...that you were pregnant."

I nodded yes to Momma Coleman and tried not to think about our baby. Instead, my thoughts went over what the police told me.

The man who killed DeWayne was a detective. They found him in his car a few miles away with a bullet in his own skull. I always wondered why people didn't just kill themselves in the first place. Why did they have to take others with them?

Momma Coleman wiped her nose. Her eyes were cherry red and her voice was hoarse.

"Momma Coleman, I can't be in here anymore... I can't…" I felt the tears coming.

We had been at the hospital all night. After the doctors tried to help DeWayne, they pronounced him dead and gave us as much time as we needed to be next to him, but I couldn't do it anymore.

I knew his kids and their mothers would want to come in, and I didn't want to be here when they came.

"I know baby... I know…"

I still had his blood on my blouse. I stood up, looking at the love of my life lying there still and lifeless. I was still not able to believe it.

"How are you going to get home?"

"I'll walk...or catch a cab." I looked down to see that I didn't have shoes on my feet. Everything had been so out of place and crazy at the house. I just wanted to get him to the hospital, and I didn't care about anything else.

"Bye, son. I love you," she said. But I couldn't do that. I knew DeWayne wasn't there anymore.

Instead, I wondered out into the hall, trying not to look at all the people with their lingering stares. I knew I looked crazy with blood all over me, my hair strewn across my head, and red eyes, but I didn't care. Tonight I almost died, and the only person close to me was now gone.

I lost my Momma and now I lost DeWayne. I was numb and I needed to rest or I was going to lose my mind.

As I walked through the lobby with Ms. Coleman on my arm, I saw her—that bitch Ariane with bloodshot eyes. Everything in me wanted to claw her eyes out, but I didn't have the strength. Besides, what would fighting with her do?

She walked towards me but I stopped her.

"Don't come close to me!" I yelled at her, startling Momma Coleman. "You can have him now." I told her as I kept walking, screaming all the way to the parking lot. "You can have him now! He's dead! You can have him!" And that was the truth.

The only man I ever loved was dead. The father of my unborn child was gone, and not even a week into marriage, I was now a widow—all over some pussy, a married woman, and a crazy ass detective who couldn't turn around.

That solidified it for me, life was way too short and I couldn't waste any more time. The love of my life was gone, and so were the best years of my life, because I couldn't walk away. I felt so stupid as I walked to my car.

The sun was coming up now, and I wondered how, on a day like today when we lost so much, the sun could rise, but that was life.

Life must go on no matter who lived or died.

Epilogue
KIARA

DeWayne has been gone a year and the tears haven't stopped. In fact, they got worse.

I stood out in the cold of the cemetery, our child in my arms, the fall leaves on the ground, saying a few words to my husband.

"He looks like you, I can see it. I wish you were here to see him."

The baby's head turned as if he saw something. Children know best when evil is near, and when I turned my head, I couldn't believe what I saw.

At the road, I saw her getting out of her car. If the baby wasn't with me, I would have charged her, slammed her to the ground, and killed her, pushing her into her final resting place in the dirt.

"I love you, baby." I said my goodbyes and headed for my car. As I got closer, our eyes locked on each other and she stopped in her tracks.

"Kiara. Hi... How are..."

"Don't talk to me. Don't you ever talk to me!" I spat the words at her as I slid my baby into his car seat.

"I just wanted to tell you I'm sorry. I didn't mean…"

I slammed the door, walking over to the bitch and getting right in her face.

"Sorry for what? Sorry for telling that bastard where I lived? Sorry for trying to steal my man after I told you to back off? Then, after finding out we were married, lying and saying you were pregnant?" The tears flowed down her face, but I didn't give a fuck about that. "Now, my son doesn't have a Daddy. And on the few days I come here to see him, you don't even have the decency to stay away."

She looked back and forth from me to the car and then to DeWayne's grave. "I didn't mean for this to happen. You had my daughter taken away from me. You told that judge to deny my custody hearing."

I looked at her sideways, trying to figure out what the hell she was talking about. "Your daughter?" I laughed at this silly bitch. "I've never said anything to any judge about you, your daughter, or anything else pertaining to you." The fact that she thought she was that important to me was stupid. Yeah, I looked into her background, checked out whatever open cases she had, but I would never try to intervene in anything like that.

"But that day, I saw you…in midtown near the court."

This bitch was crazy, like, for real crazy.

"I am a lawyer. I work in that area, you simple-minded idiot. Do you think I would do something like that?"

She nodded her head, wiping tears from her eyes, and that's when I knew it. We were all involved in a love triangle with a man who couldn't keep his dick in his pants. And if DeWayne would have been more of a man, I wouldn't have been at this cemetery right now.

"You know…this is our fault, and look at where we are now." There was nothing but the wind rustling the trees and fallen dead leaves blowing around over headstones.

"This is where men like DeWayne lead you. We spent that time on him and almost killed each other. If not physically, but mentally, we fucked each other up now look at us."

I looked in the car window at my son. He was napping now, but one day he will ask questions and I won't know what to tell him. How to explain that the decisions of me and his father left him without a parent. How do you explain to a child that his father is dead because he was fucking a married woman?

"I just... I wanted him so bad."

Ariane was crying now, but I was all cried out over DeWayne. I missed him, but our relationship was toxic. He was a sick man with issues, and that's why he couldn't stay faithful. Too bad I didn't figure those things out until I buried the man, went to counseling, and had a baby.

If I had discovered that years ago, my child wouldn't be here and maybe things would be better. But maybe it was meant to happen this way. I shook away the woulda shoulda couldas.

"I just want to be free of this bondage," Ariane said, and I agreed.

"Well, go and be free. Know that the devil may have won the battle here, but the war is over. I don't hate you anymore. I forgive you. I wish you nothing but the best." I sounded like some kind of politician, but I really meant the words. I was glad she came. At first, seeing her face dredged up all those memories and all of that hatred, but just like my psychiatrist and my pastor said, the issue lies within me. I allowed this man to drag me through the gutter, and it is DeWayne who I should have been upset with, not this woman. And in the end, I can only control me and I must forgive.

Reaching out, I extended my hand to her. She stared at my it at first, probably not sure if I would come around with my other fist and try to smash her skull in. I wanted to do it so many times, but today I was just over the bullshit and problems.

"God bless you," I said and reached my arm out further. Finally, after a few seconds, she shook my hand.

"God bless you, too."

I thought touching her would mean my hand would disintegrate into dust but nothing happened, we shook hands like two normal human beings.

It was settled. We were no longer in this imaginary ring fighting for this prized man that was really more of a dud.

"I've done a lot of things chasing a man who couldn't be a man, and now I'm done with that.."

Before I could finish, Ariane pulled me in for a hug, and as much as I didn't want to, I wrapped my arms around her. We both cried there in the road in the cemetery, cried for the loss of a person in our lives, the father of my child, my husband, and my addiction.

You see, some people are addicted to drugs, but my drug of choice was DeWayne Coleman and everything about him. I was willing to do anything to keep the man, even spend my savings, give all of myself including my sanity, and sacrifice my life. All of that to say I was his, and that now meant nothing.

"I'm so sorry," Ariane balled and so did I. I just wanted the devil to know he didn't have a claim to me anymore. I would tell my son the truth—that no matter how painful, you have to be a man of understanding and a man of integrity. Being a hoe might be fun and exciting, but it can also get you killed.

Unfortunately, I had to experience it with his father first hand.

**TEXT SOLAE
To
313131**

*For New Releases
and
Free Book Promos*

Part III

28

Kiara

Locked in his office we were supposed to be discussing business, but there was nothing more important than him being eight inches deep inside me.

"Fuck me Mr. Puzder." He liked when I called his name; rubbing his back always encouraged him and, with the g-spot procedure I just had, my pussy was tighter than a bear trap. Perfect for what I needed to do because fucking Mr. Puzder's brain's out was my key to promotion. Call it wrong, but my bank account definitely loved the investment.

"You like that, don't you?" Mr. Puzder asked. I did what I always do, I lied.

"Yes, baby. Mr. Puzder you are so big," I breathed back. I've gotten used to this life; dealing with assholes in the past, pleasing men like him has become somewhat of an art for me.

I've seen every cheater, manipulator, abuser, and straight up idiot this society has to offer. The most notorious of them all was my ex-husband. We married and I got pregnant, but my child's father was the biggest cheater I've ever been with. And yet, I loved his dirty draws.

DeWayne was my reason for waking up in the morning, and he was also the reason I cried myself to sleep. I craved that man, even with all of the bad shit that he did to me. I became addicted to the toxicity of our relationship so much so that I would do anything to keep it.

I used my money, influence, heart, soul, mouth, and, of course, my pussy to get this man to become the person I knew he could be. In the end, though, he died because he was fucking around with another woman.

A year's worth of counseling was the only thing that kept me sane after DeWayne was killed. Even now, every other Thursday, I go and sit down with my therapist to make sure I don't slip back into my old ways.

I blame my childhood for making me this way for the most part. My Mom was always trying to please my Dad, while he was running around town creating family after family. What was it about my mother that wasn't enough for him? What was it about me that didn't make him want to be a better man? I never did find out the answer and I'm not sure he could've ever given me one that would've mattered. Up until the day he died I looked for love in every man I could find, hoping to fill the void of love I lost in my father.

I loved DeWayne with that type of love and conviction until he died. I was on a peaceful mission to spread love and God's word for a while, until I took a strong look in the mirror and realized that nothing else matters in this world except pussy and money. Lucky for me, I've got them both.

"I'm coming...," Mr. Puzder announced as if I didn't already know.

"Oh yes, baby," I cooed as I rubbed his back while he

pulled out of me. His salt and pepper hair and beard sparkled as he bent down to pull up his pants.

"Damn that was good. It's like you get sweeter everyday," he smiled and I did too, but for another reason altogether.

"So what do you think about my proposal. Can I count on you?" My thoughts were on my case and the allies I needed to make some changes at the firm. Giving up my pussy was a small price to pay. He laughed as he buckled his belt and readjusted his tie.

"You don't quit, do you?," he smirked.

I didn't answer and instead made my way going to the attached bathroom where I reapplied my lipstick. I looked over my face to make sure every hair was in place, no buttons missing from my blouse. Sometimes Mr. Puzder got rough.

"Of course I don't quit," I finally replied. "That's why I'm here, right?" He laughed, but this was no joke.

"Why are you laughing?"

Coming out, the room smelled fresh again after a quick spritz of air freshener. The shades opened, looking out to the city and Mr. Puzder was no longer out of breath, sweating. It was like we'd never fucked at all.

"I'm laughing because you want me to go before the board and let you have full reign over the McGwire case."

McGwire was our biggest client and a recent renegotiation was about to be underway that would require a partner, a legal team, and a bunch of man hours to get their situation settled. I wanted the assignment badly.It was going to make my career, but getting a bunch of men to trust the newest partner was going to take more than a little persuading.

"I'm the most qualified," I quipped. "But just because I

don't have a dick between my legs you know the rest of the partners are going to fight me on this."

Mr. Puzder only laughed in return. Sitting down at his desk, I sat on the opposite side, eyeing him. His brown skin sparkled; his beard covered half of his face. He was a sort of piria of the firm; the figurative literal black sheep of the firm. But when he made a decision, the sheep usually followed. I wasn't into fucking lame ducks either. If somebody got my cookies, they were a certified boss man whether they were in the streets or running a corporation. Large and in charge is how I liked them.

"Well I think you would be a good fit. But…"

"But what?," I snapped back.

Mr. Puzder relented. "Taking the McGwire position would have you out of the office for quite some time. I would need…access to you."

I knew what that meant. He wanted to make sure he could get my pussy when he wanted it.

"You know your fiance…" he started. My blood pressure shot up at the mere mention of my other half.

"Let's not discuss him," I said.

"Why not?," Mr. Puzder pushed. "He's still in the picture isn't he?"

I wasn't naive. I never thought Mr.Puzder would leave his wife for me, and I never wanted him to him to. Plus, I had a life and ambitions to be married and give my child a father. "He is in the picture and so is your beautiful wife," I reminded him.

I eyed her picture that sat on his desk squarely, like a trophy. She was fit for her age, an undeniable beauty who was always paraded on his arm at Christmas parties.

"But where does that leave me?"

I took a deep breath as I looked into Puzder's eyes. He was getting more and more attached to me as the years went on. Our first sex romp was just a one time thing...then a year later I had to revisit the agreement, and now it was turning into once or even twice a week.

I had thoughts of love ever after and no cheating in relationships, but all of that died when I buried DeWayne. Love has its place, of course, but today those thoughts are over. I know now I want love on my own terms. I want to build success on my own and if that means I have to suck a dick or get fucked on the boss' desk, my ass pressed against the cold, slick mahogany, then so be it.

"It leaves you where you have always been," I answered. "I will take care of you, as long as you take care of me." I stared him down. He was a handsome man, but I saw him as nothing more than a pawn in my end game. I needed him to get to the other side of the board.

"Fine...I'll back you for the position, he said" I wanted to jump up and scream with joy, but the room was suddenly filled by the voice of Puzder's secretary.

"Pardon me, Mr. Puzder," she said. "But Ms. Lawrence has an appointment and her secretary asked that I buzz in to give a reminder."

"A reminder."

I pulled my phone from my suit pocket. "I don't have anything on my calendar," I said.

I knew what my day consisted of front to back and there were no meetings today besides table rocking with Chris Puzder.

"She said it's an impromptu appointment," Carmen, my secretary, went on. That happened from time to time and, with Puzder agreeing to back me, we were done with our meeting anyway.

"Fine, tell her I'm on my way please," I said.

The intercom went off and it was just the two of us again.

"Well, I'll see you at the meeting in a few days."

"Or maybe before then," he winked.

"Maybe...," I smiled but I had no intention on fucking Puzder again that soon. I had other plans for him.

Walking out of his office with my head high, I headed back across the same floor to my little slice of heaven. A corner office on the top floor with the rest of the executives. I worked my ass off to get here but as I rounded the corner my legs slowed.

The creature in my office looked familiar. My secretary knew something was wrong.he look she gave me as I approached said it all - fear to a sort of curiosity.

"Why is she in my office?," I inquired.

"Ummm Ms. Lawrence she said she needed to see you," Carmen said. "Some business matter that you apparently knew about."

I had no business with this rat bitch.

"Who is she?" Carmen was puzzled, but there was no need for such curiosity around this bitch.

"Just my deceased husband's mistress," I say to Carmen. "Call security in five minutes if we're not done."

I walked into my office, slamming the door. She jumped like a cat that had its hand in something it wasn't supposed to, and for the first time I saw the bitch who haunted my nightmares.

"Well well.... To what do I owe your visit to Ariane?" She looked the same as I remembered. She still looked broke. And cheap.

"I know I'm probably the last person you want to see," Ariane said.

"Oh...why would you think that?I love talking to the woman who fucked my husband."

I hadn't been face to face with her since that day in the cemetery.

That day I had shown restraint and humility, probably from the high of being a new mother...but right now I felt nothing but hate and rage. Everything in me wanted to kill this bitch. And there weren't many reasons why I shouldn't.

ARIANE

I took her comment and swallowed it.

"I just came here...," I started.

"To my job.," Kiara snapped. "You came to my job unannounced for what, exactly?" I rehearsed this a million times and now I hadn't been here for more than five minutes and things were already turning to shit.

"If you let me explain..." I tried.

"You have five minutes." I watched Kiara with her diamond-encrusted Rolex, Louboutin heels, and in her business suit, like she was the shit.

"Well I'm here because...," I started to explain again. This was the last place I wanted to be but I had no choice. I tried to find the words. The rehearsed reasoning for why I was here asking her for help today. I had originally wanted to tell her that I was sorry, again. I hoped that she was doing well and wanted to know how her baby was doing... but all of those words were lost on me.

"I'm waiting," she pushed. Kiara didn't make this shit easy, but I went ahead and tried to explain.

"Well, I'm not sure if you are aware of this or not...but me and DeWayne had this understanding," I said. I could see her face change as I said his name. It had been three years, and for me it still felt like yesterday. I missed him every single day.

"I know you and my deceased husband had a few understandings," Kiara snapped back.

Shit, maybe I shouldn't have said it like that.

"I mean... with my license with the state," I tried to clarify. "He was training me as his apprentice."

She laughed before I could finish my sentence.

"Apprentice? You mean, like, a dick sucking apprentice?"

"Excuse me," I shot back.

"Why are you hear ma'am?," Kiara asked. I stared at her for a second. I imagined myself jumping over her desk, slapping her face against the wall. The bitch wasn't listening to shit I was saying.

"I told you. DeWayne and I..."

"I'm going to need you to cease with saying his name," Kiara jabbed.

"Look, I'm not here to start any trouble," I insisted. "I just need you to sign something."

I pulled out the paper and slid it onto her desk, but her laugh echoed through me.

"I'm still signed on as an apprentice of your business." DeWayne had me signed on as their apprentice. The state has weird rules when it comes to stuff like that. If you sign up to be an apprentice to get a hair license, then you have to finish that program - or else give just cause why you can't.

My causes happened to include fucking the owner, getting pregnant said owner, having a miscarriage, and then, to top it all off - the owner was killed.

"I just need you to sign it," I stress. I need to be out of the program or show that I finished it. If I couldn't be signed out, I had no other choice but to spend money and time to go back to school. Time was something that I didn't have.

"Just sign...do you know where you're at girl?," said Kiara. "Do I look like a person who just signs shit?" She looked at me over some skinny wire lense glasses she was wearing. The ones like your grandma wears. Damn, she was such a corny, no-style-having bitch. All that money and she still didn't know how to accessorize and put shit together. That was why DeWayne was fucking me... he was just with this bitch for her money. He was with me because of my growth and potential. Not to mention I was a better fuck anyway. A blind man could see I was going places with the right team at my side, but he was, unfortunately, just too pussy hungry to harness my potential.

"So let me get this straight," Kiara starts. She was smiling now. "You want me to sign this paper saying you completed an apprentice program at my shop." It made my skin crawl when she said *my shop*.

"Yes," I said. "I just need that so I can officially get my license. You see, I am starting my own shop and getting my daughter…"

"Ten grand," Kiara cuts me off.

"What?," I ask.

"That's how much my signature is worth," Kiara says, smugly. This bitch had to be sick or talking in some secret language.

"If you want me to sign this, then that's what I'll need," Kiara went on. "In cash, also, no need in you getting back to your own criminal ways and trying to bounce a check."

It was official. I wanted to whoop her ass so badly, but right now I couldn't move. I was too stuck on her face, the smug grin and devilish arch of her drawn on fake ass eyebrows. I wanted to smack that look right off of her.

"I don't think you understand," I tried to further explain. "You see this was something between me and DeWayne…"

"No. I don't think you understand," Kiara said.

"DeWayne was my world." She opened her desk drawer to reveal a picture of her and DeWayne. "Before you came along, it was just me and him. We were a team and then you swooped in with your whorish ways and now my little girl doesn't have a father." She flipped around another frame of this chocolate little baby with eyes that sparkled and cheeks like her pops. She really did look like a little DeWayne.

"And instead of taking care of your own fuck ups, you decide to come bother me, *his wife*, with some bullshit you and he concocted while he was still married to me? Are you fucking serious?" Kiara was getting heated now. When she said it the shit sounded horrible but I knew in reality this was no big deal. She just needed to sign the apprentice release form... It didn't require all this dramatic ass show and tell she was hollering about.

"I was just hoping," I said.

"I was just hoping it was you that died and not him," Kiara said.

"So you're wishing death on me now?"

"I wish death on any side bitch who tries to break up my home," Kiara shouted. She threw the paper back at me when I felt hands on my shoulder.

"Ma'am, is there a problem?" A pair of rent-a-cops were standing over me like they wanted to pull my black ass up out of this office. I felt all of my days in prison come shooting back to me; all those days of listening to somebody tell me when and where to be.

"Get your fucking hands off me," I yelped.

"Get her out of here Jake," insisted Kiara. She pointed to the door. I wanted to twist her arm behind her back and shove that finger up her ass.

"I'll see you again Kiara," I said as I was dragged off. "You raggedy ass bitch." I spit on the floor. "That's why

DeWayne fucked with me. You can never be the woman I am." I really didn't want to be this way, making a scene in front of all of these people. But this bitch left me no choice.

"And make her take this with her," Kiara added. She shoved my paper towards me as the security walked me out. Back by her receptionist desk, I noticed a man who was so fine I suddenly felt weak in the knees. I stopped and stared at him. From his milk chocolate skin to his stone-like obsidian eyes, it was like he stole my soul in that instant.

"Come on ma'am, keep it going," the officers insisted. They pushed me like I was still in prison; I locked eye contact with that man and then looked away.

"Baby, what are you doing here?" Turning back I saw Kiara with her arm around some man, kissing him on the check. The way she leaned in and kissed him, I *knew* that had to be *her* man.

"Now take her down to the bottom level and see that she gets out," one of guards said to another group that was waiting for me at the elevator.

As I was escorted down to level one and made my way outside I didn't say a word. The guards gave me instructions to never come back; I snatched my document and walked out with a new mission, as I strolled down the steps to call my bestie.

" Latrice. Girl. You'll never believe what happened."

"Did she sign it."

"Hell naw," I respond.

"Damn man," Latrice starts. "I thought for sure she would sign it since that bitch was singing Kumbaya at the cemetery."

"Yeah. Well, fuck all that now," I respond. I was on a new mission.

"What you mean?"

"I'm about to do something better," I say.

"Like what?," Latrice asks. I smiled as I walked to my car trying to formulate the shit in my own brain.

"You know the dude that does promotions at Bar Olive?," I say. I knew chocolate drop from somewhere, but it took me a second to figure out why he was so familiar.

"Yeah, the fine chocolate one," Latrice says.

"Yep, that's the one."

"Okay...so what does he have to do with anything?"

I wanted to laugh at her like that bitch laughed at me in there but I held out.

"Because he is her man...," I start.

"Wait, what?-"

"...And I'm about to steal him," I finish.

In jail I learned a lot of shit. A lot. And, above all, I learned you have to respect yourself at all times. That means you and everything around you... and today Kiara violated that rule. She made the fatal mistake of showing her card and now it's time that I make my move, with her man. Again.

29

Orlando

"And make her take this with her!"

Kiara was screaming at the top of her lungs as a bunch of security guards stormed out of her office.

"Baby, what's going on?" I watched the chick they were escorting out. Little bad shorty, she reminded me of this chick I see at the club.

"It's a long story," Kiara said as she watched security damn near carry this chick away. She looked angry enough to kill, this story had to be beyond long. "Come here. You gotta calm down." I kissed her but her eyes were still following the chick as she left.

"Hold all my calls," Kiara growled at her secretary turning out of my embrace and retreating back into her office.

I had to admit this other side of her totally turned me on.

"And call housekeeping up. Tell them I need my floors cleaned."

She was a bossy bitch like that. I heard things before we got together of how Kiara liked to throw her weight around being that she was a big time lawyer. I liked the challenge; seeing her all worked up made my dick nice and hard.

As I followed her back into her office, I saw the destruction. Papers were strewn everywhere and a chair was turned over.

"Watch your step," Kiara warned. "That bitch spit on my floor."

As I looked down, I could see the glob of saliva she was talking about.

"Yo, what the fuck was that about?," I asked Kiara.

"It's such a long story O," she responded and I could hear the fatigue in her voice. My baby was tired and as her man this was my time to figure out what was hurting her and fix it, my pockets depended on it.

"I ain't got nothin' but time for you baby." I meant that. Money was time and, for mze, Kiara was a pile of money. So, listening to her was a win-win for me.

"Just...some residual shit from DeWayne," she said.

Hearing his name again made me want to throw up. I was so damn tired of hearing about this nigga. Even when he was alive I didn't like his ass, but now that the nigga was dead I hated hearing his name even more. I didn't tell her that.

"Aww baby, come here," I said, pulling her close as she started crying. She started rambling on about DeWayne, the chick who just left and how she's screwed up her life in general.

"Baby you gotta let that shit go," I tried to reassure her.

"I can't...the way he fucked me over is going to be in my soul forever," she cried. I kept patting her shoulder, wishing I could have waited until she got off to get this money.

"You can't be like that," I said. We will be walking

down the aisle in less than a month and here you are pouting about some ratchet bitch." She laughed at that.

We've done this almost every week since we got together. She would cry about her ex, something that she never knew about him or some new event. Then I would console her, give her some good dick, and get paid.

It was like I was a gigolo or some shit but when you get a bitch with money like Kiara you can't let her go. That was DeWayne's mistake and he paid for it. I'm nothing like him; first I don't fuck with just anybody and I let hoes know up front what I'm about.

"Come here baby, let me take your mind off things," I say as I pull back Kiara's jacket. And then I saw it. A bright red circle on her neck that definitely wasn't there this morning. But now, I see it like a bull's eye - the passion mark is glowing at me. "No baby...I gotta get ready for a meeting," Kiara said. She never shied away from sex with me. In her office was her favorite time. But now she was fumbling around, picking up the chair and pulling her jacket tight around her neck. I wanted to laugh at her as she started fumbling with papers on her desk,trying to avoid eye contact with me and yet I still played the game.

"Aww baby come on," I said. "I thought you liked doing it here in your office." I've kept my smile and perfect white teeth thanks to my old bitch with the great dental plan. New sparkling white veneers that put something extra on the charm I was already throwing at her. If she only knew what I was thinking in my head.

"Yeah, but I have a meeting," Kiara said. She was lying. Her receptionist already told me she was free for the afternoon. In my old life I would have slapped the shit out of her. But I was wiser now; I knew how to treat a grimey bitch like Kiara.

"But you're a partner," I said "Meetings don't get started until you get there right?"

"Yeah baby but...I gotta still do my job," she said, smiling as she reached in her desk and pulled out an envelope.

"What's this?," I said as she slid the envelope towards me.

"I was thinking,"said Kiara. "I want to contribute to that idea you had about expanding the business."

"What?" I smiled as if I didn't already know. She may have thought this was her idea, but I had been dropping subtle hints for weeks now.

"Yeah, I think I should invest in you, like how you have invested in me," she said.

Flipping open the bag, the one hundred dollar bills were crisp like they were fresh from the bank. Seeing all of those purple marks, the sign of the new hundreds, made my dick hard.

"Baby. Thank you."

Most men would have said they don't take money from their lady. Well, if she was a lady I would've agreed. The chick in front of me was nothing but a bitch and I had her card already figured out. Plus my momma always taught me not to turn down shit but my collar.

"So you take that and buy the extra equipment and machines you need," Kiara said.

"Baby, we gotta go out and celebrate this."

"I gotta get some work done and you know the baby has been sick so…"

Excuses excuses. Something was up but only if she knew I didn't give a damn just as long as she kept dropping this money on me.

"Well, aight then boo," I said, letting her off the hook. "I'll just call you when I get home from the club."

"Okay. I love you," said Kiara.

"Love you too."

I said it because I meant it. I did love Kiara Lawrence but what I loved about her was the way she was a go getter. How she had a high credit score, how she gave away her money and hooked a nigga up and, now, she was bringing me to the next level. I loved all that shit about her, everything else didn't matter.

"Alright boo, let me let you get to this meeting," I said.

She looked at me confused for a second but then she sprang back into her lie.

"Oh yeah right...Let me get my things together so I can get to the conference room," she said.

"Aight boo. Call me later."

I didn't give a fuck what she was up to. Walking out of her office, I felt like a million bucks. By the size of the stack it looked like twenty thousand dollars was in this envelope.

Outside it was like the sun was shining just for me; the birds were chirping and, to think, five years ago today I was sitting in a prison wishing that I could be here. Now I was out, a business owner with my own car and crib and, most of all, I had a bad bitch by my side who was willing to drop legal cash on me.

I wasn't letting her go, I didn't give a damn what she did and because of that I proposed to her ass and we're getting married in a little less than a month.

I was damn near floating as I walked to my car, but a phone call brought me back down.

The name on the screen said Dawn, but it might as well have said *bitch from hell.*

"Hello?"

"Hey boo." I bite my tongue to keep from yelling.

"What I tell you about calling me that?"

"What? Boo?," she questioned.

"Yeah bitch." There were some women you had to treat with loving care. Others, you called them all kind of shit to make them behave. Dawn was the latter type; she needed to be put in her place or else she was going to talk crazy.

"Bitch...Who you calling."

"Listen here," I said. "I told you not to fucking call me until you were ready to do what's right."

"But an abortion Oct...I can't do that."

"You can do whatever the fuck I tell you to do unless you want to have this baby alone." I didn't have any kids and I had it that way for a reason. And having a little gremlin by this bitch while I'm trying to get married is going to fuck up my money situation and that's something I can't have.

"But...I really want to be with you," she pleaded. It was the same words they all said.

"Bitch, if you say that one more time I'm going to hang up," I told her. "Your married, remember? I'm not fucking saving you from that."

"But…"

"But shit," I said. "I got a woman and you know that."

I could hear her sniffling through the phone. Tears probably fell down her face but I didn't give a fuck. Starting up the car I didn't say a word, I just listened in silence for a few minutes.

"Look, you're married and I'm in a relationship," I went on. "Stop fooling yourself. We can't do this long term." She took deep breaths, trying to calm down, but in my defense I don't like to lie to these hoes. I tell them the truth, they just choose not to believe it.

"But how am I going to do this," she said.

"Just go to work like usual," I explained. "Take off to

Main Chick vs Side Bitch

get the procedure done and go home. Tell him you're not feeling well." It was easy to me.

"I just...I want us to be together," Dawn continued. "If I'm leaving him, why can't we start our family now?" She was talking crazy.

"Yo, come by the club tonight and get this money," I told her. "I'm not going to tell you again that I'm not going to have no kids right now." It was simple to me. I didn't care how many times I had to say it to this broad. I wasn't fucking up what I had going.

"Okay...I'll be there," Dawn relented.

"That's my girl."

"I love you."

I looked at the phone like she was speaking another language. Without hesitating I hit the end button. There was nothing I loved about that bitch, not even her pussy. And once she aborted this baby I would be done with her ass. The only bitch I wanted in my life was Kiara and I barely wanted her. Luckily she paid like she weighed and, to me, money was better than love. At least I had never been stabbed in the back by a dollar bill.

30

Ariane

I showed up to Club XO on a Tuesday, a little later than I usually would, but I had to stand out. Not the tightest dress, I was definitely rocking the baddest one in my closet. My hair and nails were already fly, but most of all I had a purse full of money.

Not having my license had never stopped my hustle and it wasn't going to stop it now that the bitch wasn't willing to free me from the apprentice program. But what she did today put her at the top of my shit list and now that was going to have me taking her man.

I was so mad that I couldn't stop thinking about that bitch. From the time they escorted me out of that building until I got home I mapped out my plan. I made a few calls, getting more info on the man I saw today and I even had a name, Orlando. I was a bitch on a mission now and I got dressed with no panties on and an extra condom in my purse.

Now I was in the same building with Orlando Turner. He was a photographer and had a business that provided photo booths around the city in clubs and for parties. I wasn't sure if he was a paid man like DeWayne was or if he did his own thing.

I looked around for the bitch but she was nowhere in sight and a few hoes tried to talk as they got their pictures taken. A lingering hand on the shoulder here, and a laugh there, but he didn't give them any attention. He was focused, and person after person handed over payment for their pictures. A man like him making his own money made me wet, I already was going to fuck him but now I really wanted to feel that dick between my legs. Once you get introduced to a real man you can't fuck with lames... and since DeWayne I haven't been able to really fall for anyone else.

DeWayne was a real man, all about his money. Yeah he fucked with bitches here and there, but women were always attracted to the richest nigga in the room. DeWayne couldn't help that his ambitions were high.

Orlando reminded me so much of DeWayne and I hadn't even talked to him yet. I watched him from the other side of the room, trying to size him up. Word had it that he did six years in the feds, but that was cool as it only meant now we had something in common. He probably was like me and hit the ground running when he got out of jail. The streets said he started a business from an idea and now he is booming; no wonder he was there kissing that bitch Kiara... she always attracted a go getter.

"We got my man Orlando over at the picture bar. Y'all make sure you go get your picture taken."

I took that as an invitation, sliding off the bar stool I could feel a dozen eyes on me. It was always like this when I went in the club.

"Yo lil momma can I buy you a drink?" Some dread head was trying to approach me but I curved his ass. A smile and a shake of my head and I was walking past his ass towards Orlando.

"How much for a picture?" I got close enough to kiss him, blowing in his ear soft like two lovers instead of mere strangers.

"$20." He didn't waver and his eyes didn't travel past my face when he looked at me.

"Cool," I said. "I'll take give," as I handed him a fresh hundred dollar bill. I expected for that money to change his mind and at least get him to smile, but he didn't. He took my money and directed me in front of the back drop. Someone else took the pictures, a guy that was way too eager and trying to direct me like he was some kind of professional photographer.

"Look over here baby girl...Stand like this," he told me. I wasn't paying him any attention as I was too busy putting on a show for Orlando... but he was counting money.

"Is that your boss?"

"Yeah that's the boss man."

"He got a woman?" I might as well make good time and ask this lame about Orlando.

"Why? You trying to be his woman?" I didn't back away from a challenge.

"Yeah. I am." He took the pictures shaking his head at me while Orlando was talking to somebody.

"Well, here you go." He handed over the pictures in their white paper frame. "Good luck. O ain't about shit but his money."

"Oh, that's good," I replied. "Because so am I." He was talking to some dude, chopping it up as I sidled up to him.

"Excuse me. Do you own the picture booth?," I coyly asked Orlando.

He looked down at me and I felt like my feet were stuck to the floor. Now he was giving me his attention.

"Yes, is there an issue?"

"Umm..yeah I..." I coughed trying to find my words.

"Excuse me Jeff." He put his hand on my arm, guiding me away from conversation and it felt like sparks were traveling from his hand directly through to my body. "So, what's the issue?"

"I was wondering..." I forgot my plan but quickly regathered my thoughts. "I was wondering if you did parties?"

"Yeah, when is the event?"

"Soon," I said as I put my hand on his arm.

"So...what was supposed to be the problem?" *What was he talking about?*

"Problem?," I asked.

"Yeah, you said there was something wrong when you interrupted my conversation." He stood up straight, towering down at me.

"Aww I meant that..."

"You meant you wanna talk to me." Damn. He saw right through me.

"I mean, you are sexy." He ran a hand down the back of his head licking his lips as I said it.

"Yeah, I know that." And he was conceited. "And you are too. But you don't want to talk to me."

"Why?" I asked, confused.

"Because I make pretty bitches like you crazy...no offense." I didn't know if I was offended or intrigued by the challenge.

"Oh, none taken baby," I said. "But you see you've never had anything like me." I felt like we were in battle instead of inside the loud club. I could have sworn we were all alone instead of having a few hundred people crowded around us.

"That's what you think, huh? So what are you...if I've never had anything like you before?" It was time for me to show and tell now. I thought of an answer, but I was just going to blurt it out.

"Come here...let me tell you in your ear." He looked hesitant at first but he eventually bent down. I didn't say a word, instead I ran my tongue over his earlobe and nibbled on it for a quick second.

"Oh...that's what type of girl you are?," he asked, standing back up. I was about to answer as I had a clever comeback all planned out when I heard the glass shatter and screams start. I turned around to see more glass breaking and a loud popping sound that was like an explosion. It didn't take long for me to realize it was a gun, and an even shorter time before I hit the floor.

31

Dawn

Dawn Powell parked a block away from the club like she always did on the nights that Orlando had to work.

She knew the rules. He already told her that he didn't want her in the club bothering him when he was working, but tonight she didn't feel like playing the role of car lurker. Instead she got out, dressed good enough to kill a room full of super models. She was beautiful; long legs, flowing black hair and a perfect size nine, but the baby made her feel like her dress was a size too tight.

Dawn wasn't 'that' pregnant, just a mere six weeks... but to her it felt more like six months.

Nevertheless she walked down to the club, her eyes on the line that wrapped around the building. She used to stand in that line waiting to get in and gawking at the people who skipped the line but now she was one of the skippers. It was an easy perk obtained from fucking the club photographer. Getting to the door Dawn smiled at the security guards, thinking they would return the favor... but instead their faces were hard as stone.

"Damn y'all. What's wrong? Somebody steal ya girl?"

She laughed, making a joke like usual, but tonight they didn't laugh back. They only looked at each other, silently trying to figure out who was going to carry out the order that Orlando gave them at the beginning of the night.

One guy spoke up, his belly poking out way past his chest on his tall frame.

"Yo Dawn, we can't let you in."

"What?"

"Yeah, we got orders."

"Orders?"

"Yeah we can't let nobody skip no more so you gotta get in line."

"This shit don't sound right. Is O in there?"

They all looked at each other again.

"Naw he's gone," somebody piped up. but that also sounded like a lie.

"So he's not in there." Craning her neck from side to side she tried looking over the towering security but that was damn near impossible.

"Naw he ain't here."

"Yeeah….whatever." She walked towards the back of the line or so they thought. Instead, Dawn looped around the building towards the back patio and looked inside. Her view was perfect, seeing Orlando after only a few seconds of peering inside.

She called him as she stared inside, the phone up to her ear and her other hand on her hip. It had to be a mistake; maybe the security had her confused with someone else. But as his phone rang Dawn watched as the man she loved looked at his cell phone and sent her to voicemail. Not once, but twice. She was ready to scream when she saw a woman walking towards the booth. She could tell by the body language that the chick was flirting.

"That's why you don't want me in there. Yo dawg

ass…" Dawn stomped away, her feet moving as fast as her thoughts. Making it around the corner to an open lot she saw his car tucked back into his usual parking spot.

Do it. A part of her was directing her thoughts. But before her good side could stop it her hand was already digging around her purse, pulling out a retractable knife. The blade came out in the touch of a button and before Dawn could stop herself she was pushing the knife into Orlando's tires.

"So you wanna play games with me." Just a few slashes and all of the air leaked out of O's tires in seconds. "I'm carrying your baby and this is how you treat me." The blade was back down but Dawn was only getting started.

She walked to her car counting all the things she had done for Orlando. Sending him messages while he was in jail, getting him set up with a place when he got out of prison and, of course, giving him every hole on her body for his sexual pleasure.

"And this is the thanks I get." At her car Dawn was breathing harder than a marathon runner but she had no intention of calming down. She started her ride and made a u-turn in the street circling back towards the club. Parked across the street she saw clear into the club, Orlando was there near the front now talking to some chick. Her arm on his and the smile on her face made Dawn almost vomit.

"Fuck this." Popping open her glove compartment the Chrome 380 came out, the safety off and her trigger finger fitting firmly in place. Dawn was better with a gun than she was with a knife. Aiming for the top windows of the club she took a single breath right as she squeezed the trigger.

Bullseye.

The window shattered, people screamed and ran, but she kept shooting. One window after another until she saw Orlando was no longer in deep conversation. She wasn't sure where he went but there were people everywhere. Throwing her gun on her passenger seat she took off like everyone else. But unlike them, Dawn wasn't afraid. Guns didn't scare her and neither did the thought of anyone seeing. What terrified her the most was losing Orlando, her man, and the father of her child.

"We're about to have a family and you do this?" She shook her head as she drove home.

"Well it's my choice and I'm not getting an abortion," she said to no one but the inside of her car. It was the rehearsed speech of what she was going to tell Orlando tonight to reason with him about the unborn seed growing in her stomach.

Now, after what she saw, there was no reasoning. It was her choice and she was keeping this baby and she would have Orlando all to herself. Even if that meant she would have to slash a few more tires and empty more hot lead from her gun. Either way he would be her's. That was a promise and a threat, all rolled into one.

32

Orlando

The glass broke and and fell down to the ground, getting everywhere. But I rather get falling glass on me than a bullet to the head.

I covered old girl up out of instinct, my body on top of hers waiting for the bullets to stop and eventually they did. But it was too late, everyone was already starting a stampede out of the club.

"Come on. Get up." I pulled her to her feet. Not sure why, but her shaking body and screams under me made me feel like I had to protect her.

"Oh my God...Oh my God."

"Larry you aight?," I screamed to my worker.

"Yeah..." He looked like none of this shit fazed him. "You want me to stay and work or pack it up?" Looking around, the club was in chaos. The music had stopped and everyone was heading for the door. Before I could answer the lights came on.

"Naw man, pack that shit up. I'll get straight with you tomorrow."

"Aight." This was nothing to us, gunshots and niggas

scrambling... but what I needed to know was where was this shit coming from. I had enough heat on me, and niggas shooting at this club had never happened before. Something told me Link had his fingers all over this shit.

"Yo Turo. What the fuck is going on."

"Man some fucking car drove by busting."

"Was it Link and them niggas?"

"Shit I'm not sure." That was all I needed to hear. "Yo I'm out." I gave him a five but looking down I noticed old girl was still holding on to me like I was her man.

"Yo baby girl, you gotta let me go."

"Shit...I'm sorry. I just..." The tears were streaming down her face. She didn't have to say it. Those were tears of somebody that has been around gun fire a time or two and it must not have ended well.

"It's okay, you're okay. I'm okay. Let's get you to your car. Come on." I didn't wait for an answer, taking her hand as I lead her through the maze of people to a side door. My car was a few feet away.

"I'll take you to your car. What's your name?"

"Ariane." Her voice was shaky just like her hands.

"It's cool, Ariane. We're safe now okay." She agreed with me as I walked with her; other people were burning rubber and running, but I already knew that whoever it was had to be long gone. It was nobody but Link who did this shit and he was only trying to send a message.

He wanted his money and I wanted to give it to him, but I had other shit I needed to do first.

"Here, there is my car right there." I hit the alarm but something didn't look right. Getting closer my car looked a few feet lower to the ground.

"Is that your car with the flat tires?"

"What?" I looked closer. The tires were flat as a fucking pancake.

"Ain't this a bitch." I touched the rubber feeling the slashes. Deep gashes that weren't a mistake, every single tire had at least two.

"Man, what the fuck!" I looked around, my pistol getting hot on my waist. I wanted to pull it out, bust a few shots on my own but that wouldn't have helped shit.

"My car is right over there."

"Naw, I'm gonna call a tow." Just as I said it thunder hit the sky. She jumped like it was more gun shots but quickly the thunder was followed up by a few sprinkles. I didn't give a fuck about no little bit of rain, but that would only mean it would be hours before the tow truck got here.

"Shit it's raining."

"My car is over there. Come on." She pulled me, her hand in mine like I was her man. I followed her, damn near running to her car. We got in just in time for the sky to open up and throw down a monsoon of rain.

"Damn man. I didn't know it was supposed to fucking rain."

"Shit neither did I." She looked cute in the dim light of the car. I expected to see makeup pouring down her face or weave tracks slipping out of her hair, but she looked all natural.

Wiping her face with a napkin, I didn't see any color. With a few fingers through her hair she pulled it back into a ponytail. I could tell by the way she went down to her scalp and pulled her hair back that it was all hers. That shit turned me on, and that's when I saw it.

"Wasn't you at the law office earlier today?"

"Law office?"

"Yeah, today."

"Oh yeah...I was there looking into some business about getting my daughter back."

"Word..."

"Yeah...long story." She said turning on the car. "So, you gonna call a tow truck?"

"Naw, can you just take me to my crib. I don't stay far. I'll get my other car and come back."

"Damn, you got two cars?"

"Yeah, every man needs a work vehicle and a personal vehicle." She smirked at that nodding her head.

"What? You ain't never heard that before."

"Naw, I just… well. Maybe I haven't heard it before." I wanted to laugh, but a part of me was still pissed about my ride.

"I figured that. You probably used to dealing with some busta ass niggas. I'm anything but that." I smoothed off my clothes as the thunder crashed lightening up the sky.

"Well, you must be used to dealing with some petty ass bitches."

"Why you say that?"

"Because. Only a petty bitch would slash some tires." She eased away from the curb as I thought about her words.

"A bitch…" She nodded. "Really?"

"Yeah, think about it. If you had some beef with somebody, why would they slash your tires like a punk? That's something a bitch would do."

That made sense. Checking my phone, there were no missed calls from Link but at least ten calls from Dawn.

"Where am I going?" I told her to make a few turns and where we were going.

"Yo, I didn't get to ask. What is your name?" She smiled at that and I could see the white of her teeth in the dark.

"It's Ariane remember…"

"Oh yeah. That's right. Damn. My bad."

"Yeah, I know you probably come into contact with a

lot of bitches. But I'm different. You remember that." I laughed at that. She had a lot of mouth, I could tell that she was a handful but lucky for her my hands were free at the moment.

I watched her drive, listening to the rain beat against her car and I knew it right then. I was going to fuck the shit out of this chick tonight.

33

Ariane

His house wasn't just nice, the shit was upscale. He had to be rich. Not what I was expecting at all. I parked in the garage right next to an E-class Benz and I knew it was official. This dude had some money.

"Damn, so this is all you."

"Yep." I didn't have any words as the garage door lowered down behind us as the sound of the rain outside intensified.

"Shit, maybe I should get going?"

"In this...Naw. Just come in for a minute until it stops." He was reading my mind. I wanted to come in. I was dying to see his house but after that shit at home I was also dying to get to the crib. I tried to avoid shit like this and after DeWayne I was in no mood to be around stupid shit.

"You see that was why I don't go to clubs." Walking in his house all the lights were out.

"Shit I think the power is out."

"Damn..." I couldn't see much, but what I did see looked nice.

"And you live here by yourself?"

"Yeah," Orlando said.

"So no chick is going to pop out…"

"I'm a grown man. I don't play that shit." He shut me right up.

"I'll be right back. Gonna go check the circuit breaker."

"Okay…" He left me alone in the living room. Only a picture of a lion hung on his wall, dark colored furniture and a glass coffee table and a huge book shelf on the wall. No TV, no coasters, no shoes laying across the floor, and no dirty clothes hanging off of the couch.

I heard a click and the lights were back on. Sure enough I saw everything and it all looked in place.

"It was just the circuit breaker. Happens sometimes when it rains." Back in the room under the full lights I could barely look at him. He looked so damn good, I just looked away pretending to be preoccupied with his book shelf.

"I can go ahead and leave now. Rain isn't…." The thunder crashed again like God was trying to keep me here.

"It's cool. Just chill," he insisted. You want something to drink. I got some wine."

Shit… I was supposed to be down for this but I wasn't expecting this type of man. He was different, he was grown up for real. I hadn't fucked with somebody on their shit like this, not even DeWayne had his own shit. This had to be something else going on.

"Umm, yeah that's cool." He was back in a few minutes with wine glasses and a full bottle of wine.

"This is Red Moscato. Hope you like it."

"Damn…"

"What?"

"I mean…you just."

"I just what?," Orlando asked.

"You're not what I thought." He smiled at that. "What were you thinking I was?" I couldn't answer that question the way I wanted to. I wanted to tell him I thought he was the drone boyfriend of that bitch Kiara... but he was already answering for me.

"You thought I was one of those live with ya momma type niggas huh?" I had to laugh, I actually ran into a lot of guys that lived with their momma's until the momma croaked or finally threw they grown asses out.

"Yeah. I guess I was."

"See I told you I'm not what you're used to." He poured the wine.

"Well, don't be so sure."

"Whatever. Let's have a toast."

"To what?"

"To me fucking you." I almost choked.

"What?"

"That's what you want to toast to?"

"Yeah. I mean it's the truth."

"Wow, your really fucking conceited." Either I got shot and I was dead, or this guy was so fucking fine that he felt that confident to say shit like that to me.

"I'm just telling the truth."

"You don't even know me. What do you mean telling the truth?" Clinking his glass on mine he sipped the wine as I watched the glass press against his full, plump lips. Lips that could probably suck the clit right off my body. Lips that were probably experts at licking nipples and tasting me until I screamed his name.

Something about a confident man turned me all the way on and the perfect aphrodisiac was rumbling outside.

"You see. I knew you wanted to fuck me from the club.

But usually women like you are too afraid to fuck a man on the first date."

"Correction sir. This is not a date." I sipped my wine as he cleared his throat readjusting himself.

"Excuse me. A first meeting of someone," Orlando corrected himself.

"So, you respect women that fuck men when they first meet them?"

"Yeah why not." I nodded to what he was saying, sizing him up. Looking at the tattoos on his arms wondering where the wonderful art lead. I hoped it went all the way up his arms and landed on his chest.

"Because. Most men think that is indicative of a hoe." I sipped more of my wine trying to make a good decision. Did I want to give in tonight or string this out for longer?

"You see, I keep telling you I'm not like most men."

"So you say…," before I could finish the lights went out again.

"Fuck it. I'm gonna leave them off." I didn't flinch as he inched closer to me.

"You ever heard of St. Louis?" I asked him taking slow sips.

"Yeah, in Missouri right?"

"Bingo."

"What about it?"

"You see. I was going to explain that I'm from the *show me* state." I inched closer to him.

"And what does that mean?" Leaning in right in front of those pussy sucking lips of his I was nose to nose with him.

"That means…I'm from the show me. And all of that talk doesn't mean shit. I want you to show me…" Before I could finish those same lips were on me. His tongue was parting my lips and was in my mouth, exploring.

His hands were pulling my clothes to his hot body; I wanted him, every molecule of my soul wanted him inside me.

"Show you huh," he talked as he kissed me. Tasting my lips and pulling at my clothes and after a few seconds he pulled away.

I was breathing hard, trying to put down my wine glass when he stood up pulling off his shirt. With the streetlight peeking through his blinds I only got a faint glimpse of his chest but I was right. Those tattoos on his arms did run up to his chest and down his stomach.

"Well I guess Ms. Show me. I'm going to have to do just that." I gulped down the rest of the wine as he got down on his knees, pulling me to the edge of the couch I couldn't take a breath before his head was between my legs. My bare pussy was fully exposed to him, his beard tickled between my thighs but his tongue tickled even more. He ran his tongue up my thigh to my pussy lips and circling around.

"Shit…"

"Is that enough showing for you…Ms. Show me…"

"Please, don't stop," I said.

"What?"

"PLEASE DON'T STOP."

"Oh…I don't stop. Not until the job is done." His lips ran across my pussy again as he pulled me so close I felt his breath on my clit.

"But you see, I also don't take nicely to being told what to do." I didn't know what to say to that, there was nothing to say. I felt him getting up, pulling me up with him. But just as soon as I was on my feet he was turning me around and pushing me back down on the couch.

"Doggy style…Get on your knees over the couch." I did

as he said. I felt like I was going on a secret field trip to a land far away.

"Okay...I" He pulled up my dress, my ass meeting the coolness of the room. Then the warmth of his tongue and the tickle of his beard.

"Oh shit...yes," I moaned. I didn't mean to moan. I wasn't usually a moaner but getting your pussy ate from the back will do strange things to a woman. He grabbed my ass like it was an old friend that he hadn't seen in years. As he sucked my pussy he moaned with every lick.

"Ohh, you taste so good." It was like my pussy was a candy apple or a ripe peach and he was starving for me.

"Damn...damn boy." I was right, he was a pro with his tongue. Slow licks followed by fast then slow again. He knew just where to touch me, pulling me and pushing just hard enough for me to know he was there but not hard enough to hurt me. Usually men never got that shit right, but Orlando was a pro.

"Say my name."

"Or-lan-do" He slapped my ass making me yelp in pain but my pussy tingled from the pleasure.

"Say it!"

"Orlando." Another slap sent my pussy to a seizure.

"LOUDER!"

"Orlando!"

"Yeah. That's how you say it. Show me." He laughed as I moaned, licked my pussy as I came and shuddered all over his couch but he wasn't done.

He cupped my legs and before I knew it he was holding me upside down, his face still between my legs.

"Oh my God..." an upside down sixty nine was only something I saw on TV but as he lifted me up I saw his dick right in front of my face. He didn't have to tell me what to do,

I took it in, swallowing him whole. He wasn't going to out-do me, this motherfucker wasn't going to be fine as fuck, paid, and fuck the shit out of me without me making him cum too.

He slurped me up as I licked. The blood rushing to my head made me dizzy but I didn't care. I was getting my pussy ate by a man that could have a PhD in clit licking.

He was devouring me and I was doing the same to him. His hands clutched around my waist holding me like I weighed just two pounds. I was wetter than I had been in years, my pussy was jumping like never before and as much as I tried to push it to the side, my heart was beating fast but not from the sex. From what I felt, the way he cared for me in the club wasn't no straight gentleman shit. I knew when somebody was straight digging me and what he did was on that level. The same way DeWayne used to look out for me.

"Shit...I'm cumming. I'm cumming." I hummed with his dick pulsating in my mouth. He didn't stop, he kept going as he pumped his hips into my face.

Orlando was right, he wasn't no regular nigga. No regular nigga could make me cum two times in one night. It was official, Kiara was never getting this nigga back.

I was keeping him for myself.

34

Kiara

Trying to get dressed for work, I had a million things shooting through my mind. This new case, the house I was having built, but most of all I was thinking about this wedding. Close to two hundred thousand dollars was being spent to bring me and Orlando together. This photography empire we are building would make that back in a month when we get the new photo equipment up in every club in the city and this wedding was going to be the kickoff to all of that.

I don't necessarily love Orlando, I highly like him and consider him a great choice for a husband but loving him was never in my plans.

After DeWayne died I said I would never love another man. This marriage was about business. I could control Orlando and he came with enough drive that would have me rich. He knew how to play his role and that's what you need in a mate when you are about to become one of the first black prosecuting attorney's in the District. That was my end plan and from there I would become a judge. But I couldn't do that without a husband, even though my future husband did have a background, in today's climate that would only prove to help me.

"There was a shooting last night at a nearby club." I whipped my head around trying to see which club it was.

Sure enough it looked like one of Orlando's spots. Shot up like usual with a crowd of police and what seemed like several broken windows.

"No one was hurt but the police are still looking for suspects." At least everyone was okay but nine times out of ten they would never figure out who was responsible.

"This shit has to stop." I must have been talking too loud because no sooner than I said the words I heard the footsteps, small and fast beating on the hardwood floor to my door.

"Mommy…" my little baby was coming towards me.

"Mommy, do you think Daddy can see us from Heaven?" These were the questions I woke up to.

"Yes baby, he can see us. He's watching over us and he is really proud of you." I told my son this every morning. He always asked the same thing and even though he never met DeWayne I told him all about his dad. DeWayne's pictures lined his room, and his name resembled his father's. It didn't matter who I was marrying, DeWayne would always be his father and I needed him to know that and to always remember him.

"C'mon DeAndre let's get you ready for school." But my son was too busy jumping around on the empty side of my bed. The side where no man slept because I wasn't interested in letting him see a bunch of neanderthals bounce around my bed until I was joined in marriage with somebody.

That is the price I pay as a single mother and if it meant I went to sleep in a cold bed then so be it.

Luckily it wouldn't be that way much longer, this time

next month I couldn't believe that I would be married. Until then, me and Orlando kept our own houses. He lived on the other side of town and I kept my house with DeAndre. It was better that way because I didn't want to go and get my baby confused so instead I kept my routine normal. With the help of a nanny I kept things pretty much intact.

But my nanny was my lifeline. Working late and having to be gone for a couple of days at a time I felt safe leaving her with DeAndre so I could live my life.

"There you are." Looking up I saw Dawn. She looked tired today. Extra set of bags under her eyes.

"DeAndre go do like mommy taught you. Go brush your teeth and I'll be right there." Dawn was in DeAndre's room folding clothes but I could tell she had been crying.

"Everything okay Dawn?"

"Yeah...everything's fine." She put on a fake smile but she avoided eye contact with me. Rule number one in being a lawyer is that I had to become an expert at spotting a liar. I could easily do it with people that I wasn't romantic with so, seeing Dawn's lie was easy.

"C'mon you can tell me. I'm not just your boss. We gotta be cool and communicate, remember." She took a deep breath, a faint smile coming over her face as I saw her relax.

"Well, remember that guy I was telling you about?"

"Oh no...not him again. The one with the gambling problem." She nodded sheepishly.

"I wanted to break it off...but...I found something out." This crap was like a soap opera. First she tells me she meets this guy. He is in and out of a relationship with some woman and then the layers of this guy start unraveling. From gambling debts to other woman outside of the chick that she knew about.

"Dawn, I thought I told you that your employment was

going to rely on you staying away from this guy?" I didn't want any confusion or bs around DeAndre. Dawn was young, impressionable, and I could see something happening like her doing something against her morals to keep this creep.

"I know...and I'm sorry but..." She rifled through her pockets and pulled out a pregnancy test.

"Oh my God..." It was like a bad dream. It was the same shit I went through with DeWayne and now she was making the same mistakes that I had.

"I found out a few days ago."

"And what did he say?" She wiped her crying eyes as she tried telling me the story.

"He said he's getting married to the other chick."

"Really? So where does that leave you and your baby?"

She shrugged. "I'm not sure. He wants me to get an abortion."

"Jeez Dawn." This was bad, very bad and I couldn't hide it.

"But what about your husband?" There were more layers to this than an onion; it stank and made you cry.

"He's still overseas. He has no idea. He won't be home on leave for months." The other side of the coin was that Dawn was married. Not a happy marriage, but a marriage nonetheless. She stayed for the money and her husband was overseas fighting for the country. Who sends divorce papers to a man on deployment?

"You gotta get this fixed." I gave her an eye, that told her everything she needed to know about my thoughts. "I've told you about my history. Take it from me you don't want to go down that road."

"I know but...this guy...he is my world and I don't want to lose him." Dawn said and it sounded like a younger and dumber me. I tried to think of better wording but I could tell she wasn't trying to get rid of this man. Sitting on the bed DeAndre came bumbling into the room showing his teeth to me.

"Look mommy...All done!"

"That's great, baby. Here, put on these clothes that Ms. Dawn put out for you and I will be right back." Taking Dawn's hand I lead her into my bedroom.

"Okay. You love him but you have a child inside of you. You have to love yourself." She nodded tears still flowing. "I advise you to leave this man alone. Get an abortion, Dawn and get on with your life."

She nodded wiping her eyes but I could tell the words were going in one ear and out of the other.

"But what about this chick he's supposed to be marrying?"

"What about her?"

"Should I tell her?" I thought about Ariane when she said that.

"No, she probably already knows. You should leave her out of it." Dawn nodded.

"Look, I'm going to take care of this and I promise I'm not going to put my job in jeopardy," Dawn says.

"Good, because I need you around here. Especially when me and Orlando go on out honeymoon." Jamaica for two weeks with my husband. We were going to put down a solid plan for integrating our lives and give me some alone time after this blow up that was about to happen. I made a decision and things needed to change at work, and what I had in mind was sure to cause an explosion.

"Don't feel bad. I was like you. Young and dumb once, you will get over this...Shit I'm already late. I still have to get these invitations to Orlando so he can mail them out."

"Oh I can do that."

"Really?" All smiles... it was like Dawn wasn't even crying a few minutes ago.

"Yeah no problem."

"Dawn, you're a lifesaver. Thank you! Just use the credit card I gave you at the post office and bring me back the receipt."

"No problem," says Dawn. "That's what I'm here for. To make your life easier." I wanted to hug her, tell her that she meant the world to me but my phone ringing stole my thoughts.

"I gotta go. This is my boss." Scrambling out of my bedroom I answered the phone as business-like as I could, even though I knew at this time of the a.m. it was nothing but pleasure on Mr. Puzder's mind.

"This is Ms. Lawrence," I answer.

"Damn, I wanna fuck you." He had no idea who was around me or even if he was on speakerphone or not.

"Excuse me sir. Hold on a moment." I muted the phone and handed it to Dawn for a moment.

"Come give mommy a hug DeAndre." He sprang from his room and hugged me so tight like he would never see me again.

"Love you Mommy."

"Love you too little man."

"Have a nice day at work." He was so grown running off and leaving me. His love gave me so much strength. Like everybody else in my life they wanted something from me, but he loved me just because. For him I knew exactly what I needed to do.

"Thanks Dawn. I'll see you later." Taking my phone back I unmuted it, pressing an additional button that sent the recording of the call into effect.

"Okay, I apologize. What can I do for you Mr. Puzder?"

"You know what you can do," he answered. "You can come suck my dick before I go into this meeting." I walked downstairs listening to him tell me all the ways he wanted to fuck me and in what positions.

"Don't you think it's a little early to be talking like this sir."

"It's never too early for me to slide my dick inside that sweet wet pussy of yours," he answered.

"Sir, I don't think this is appropriate." He laughed falling right into my plan. Grabbing my keys I made my way to the garage and Mr. Puzder dug deeper into his own grave.

"Inappropriate. Look bitch. Don't get a moral compass and fuck around and lose your job."

Bingo, that was exactly what I wanted him to say.

"Are you threatening me sir?"

"Hell yeah I am. I got you to where you are today. If you want to stay there stop with this amnesia act you are putting on. Get to this damn office so I can bust a load on one of those brook brothers suits you like wearing. You know...the thousand dollar ones that you can afford because I made you a partner."

It was like stealing candy from a baby. Starting the car and backing out of the driveway I played it all cool.

"I apologize sir," I said. "You know my job is the most important thing to me."

"What the hell is wrong with you this morning? Quit playing and get in here pronto."

"Yes sir. Right away." He was hanging up before I could finish my sentence but it was perfect. The damage was done. I pushed a button to end the recording and without even blinking I opened up my email, attaching the recording and sending it straight to my HR manager.

Please listen to this privately and get back to me.

I sent the message with a smile. I was done playing with Puzder. Yeah I fucked him all these years to get what I wanted and I guess he assumed that I would be his secret work concubine for the rest of my life.

This was only part one in my plan. In the next few weeks there would be a shit storm and, of course, I would be landing on top like always.

35

Orlando

The rain stopped and my phone was ringing off the hook. I had to face a lot of shit that I wasn't ready for, but the one that took the cake had to be Dawn. It was the messiest shit I've ever done. Fucking the bitch that played nanny to my step son and now she was pregnant. My tires were slashed and ole girl was right; that was nothing but a jealous bitch move... but I had that bitch under control. She was going to get that abortion even if I had to buy a vacuum and suck the baby out myself.

But, for now, I just needed to lay low and stack my money. As soon as I say 'I do' to this bitch I'm going to be paid like Rockefeller so I just had to play my position and keep this bitch quiet for now.

There were only two things that could get my mind off of my stupid mistakes. Pussy and poker. I had conquered the first distraction last night, fucking this chick that was now lying on my chest, but now my poker hand was itching and my phone was ringing. All shit that was making it hard for me to lay here in this bed.

"Yo whatup," I answered the phone pushing my house

guest off to the side. She was naked and her ass was poking out from under the sheets.

On any other day I would have fucked the shit out of her once again but it was daylight. I needed to get up and get to the money.

"Yo man, we got a problem." It was my man Alonzo on the line.

"What's that?"

"That game last night got intercepted," he said. That meant we got robbed. But worst of all, it wasn't our money.

"Intercepted," I said. "By who?"

"I have no idea," he responded. "We trying to figure that out now but we owe that nigga Tommie another five stacks." Shit...I wanted to punch a hole in the wall but I took a deep breath instead.

"Okay, we need to get some more games scheduled."

"With what money?" Only thing I had at my disposal was the money that Kiara gave me for the new equipment.

"I got a few bands we can work with."

"Okay. Get it to me asap so I can get shit rolling and buy us some time with Tommie." That eased part of me ,but now Kiara was blowing up my line.

"Aight let me take care of something and I'll be at you in a few."

"Aight." I clicked over to Kiara as my house guest turned over looking straight up at me.

"Hey boo."

"Baby you okay?"

"Yeah I'm good. Why wassup?"

"I've been calling you then I saw there was a shooting at the club." That was the last thing I needed was for Kiara to start getting nervous.

"Aww naw baby that's just the media blowing things out of proportion."

"So there wasn't a shooting?" I didn't want to say there wasn't so I did the best I could to spin it around.

"Well, some cats were shooting but the windows got broken from the storms." She laughed at that.

"Wow, I tell you the media tries to twist shit around all the time."

"Yup, so what you doing?"

"On my way to see you." I felt my heart drop to my feet.

"Aww yeah."

" Psych. I wish. I'm on my way to the office. Got a meeting with HR this morning."

"Aww yeah about what?"

"Well, partly about that hag who came to my office yesterday."

"Yeah what was that about?," I asked. She was sitting up in the bed now, looking at me. I wondered- did she think I really bought that explanation she had about me seeing her at Kiara's office yesterday? I never forget a face and I definitely don't forget an ass.

"She's one of DeWayne's old side bitches. She wanted to come ask me for a favor and I told that bitch no. I don't do shit unless money is involved."

"True dat baby. That's crazy."

"Well, I gotta go," she said. "I was going to tell you to drop by the house and grab the invitations but I'm going to have Dawn send them off." Just hearing Kiara say her name made me nervous. I had to get rid of that bitch.

"Baby, when you gonna fire Dawn?"

"Oh my God boo I was thinking about it this morning," Kiara said. "She told me that she was pregnant." I broke out in an instant sweat. Ducking back into the bathroom I sat on the edge of the tub listening to all the shit Dawn had to say to my woman about this mystery man AKA ME! Only if Kiara knew the truth she probably would have tried to cut my balls off and feed them to me. But I played dumb.

"So, she told you all that."

"Yeah, before I left out this morning," Kiara told me.

"So...what she gonna do?"

"Hell, I don't know," she said. "I just need her to hold out until after our honeymoon then I'm going to get rid of that bitch." I needed her to get rid of Dawn ASAP. But if I learned nothing from the old school pimps I knew that you couldn't just cut off a bitch. You had to make them cut themselves off.

"Boo, I'm pulling into the garage at work. I'm gonna call you back."

"Okay baby. Love you."

"Love you too." I hung up with the woman and I had to really rethink some shit. I had to get the poker games back up and going to get my money back and I had a bitch I needed to get rid of. And in the meantime I had another bitch in the other room. Opening the door she was just as naked as when I left her. Laying on her stomach, she was playing on her phone.

"Good morning!"

"Morning. How are you?" She was trying to be sweet but there was nothing sweet about this bitch but her pussy.

"I'm confused," I started. "You said you were up at the law office about some business." She tensed up. "You see, before you tell me a lie I want you to know I'm not like any nigga that you ever fucked with." Sitting up on the bed with her legs folded she looked like a kid who was about to get a whooping.

"I was there on business," she said.

"With who?"

"Kiara Lawrence."

"Hmmm. So you're the chick who was fucking with DeWayne that she told me about," I replied.

"One of a few, I'm sure," she said. I had to agree with that. What I knew about that nigga DeWayne would fill up a book and the main thing was he kept a few hoes.

"So let me guess," I said. "You saw me and recognized me from the club and tried to come in last night and start some shit." She wanted to smile; I saw the smirk trying to crease across her face but she kept it in check.

"Not exactly," she said.

"So what the fuck is it then?"

"Honestly?" She asked.

"I wouldn't have it no other way."

"That was my mission but then after spending time with you I decided I'm really drawn to you," she explained. "I just don't know why you fucking with Kiara." I wanted to laugh in this bitch's face. She was drawn to me after a few minutes of my time? She had to be smoking or something.

"Me being with Kiara is my business" I snapped. "I'm going to marry her and whatever little scheme you had up your sleeve ain't gonna work." She looked sad like a fucking puppy.

"So get ya shit and go ahead and leave."

"No.."

"No? What the fuck?"

"I mean...I understand that's your woman and I respect that," she said. "I just...I know you are real. I know you're something special and even if I gotta play second to that bitch...I will." She stood up from the bed, walking towards me.

"So you just want to be in the fold."

"Yep."

"Even though I just told you I'm getting married in about three weeks," I said again.

"Yes." She dropped to her knees, my dick was still hard and she pulled him from my boxers and into her jaws, but I stopped her after a few sucks.

"Well, if you down for the team then I need some cash."

"Whatever you need. I got you." She kept eye contact with me as she swallowed my dick into her mouth. At that moment I knew this bitch was the real deal; that's why DeWayne fucked with her, and most of all that's why I wasn't about to let her ass go.

IT TOOK me the better part of the day to get out of bed with that bitch Ariane. She licked me from my head to my toes and then back up again. I could see why that nigga DeWayne kept her on the team but most of all she tossed a nigga a few bands before she left.

Who knows what the bitch was up to but I was only down to get this bread, so none of that shit mattered to me anymore. I already got a tow truck to pick up my ride and was en route to my niggas so we could get our games back on the road.

Pulling up to the spot from the outside, it looked like a legitimate corner store with food, sodas, and candy. But around the back and in the basement we ran one of the best illegal gambling halls in the city.

Our moneymaker was poker but we did everything from craps to roulette. Walking into the store I gave a few niggas high fives and shakes as I eased my way into the back. Once behind the 'employees only' door it was only a few feet until I hit the steps to the basement where all the real money was made.

But a part of the business was borrowing money from motherfuckers you didn't want to. And sometimes, like last night, there was a robbery. It's all kinds of pits and falls in this business but for a nigga like me that came from nothing I can't help but want to have my hands in everything, no matter the risks.

Going back to being broke wasn't an option for me but I would risk it all to keep being my own boss. I couldn't be told what to do by no nigga. That's why we needed to get this money and pay Tommie back.

"Wassup boi," I gave Alonzo a five as I looked around at the room. Chairs were turned over and shit looked straight crazy.

"Tell me what happened bruh?"

"Man two niggas came in towards the end of the night," he said. "Ski masks and 40 Cals."

"What they hit us for."

"All of it. 140k."

"FUCK!" I couldn't help but scream. That was pretty much everything and then some.

"And you know that nigga Tommie don't give a fuck. He wants his cut no matter what."

"Damn man."

"So you got that cake to give to Tommie. If you don't, we done."

"Damn man." Pulling out the money Alonzo looked like he saw a ghost.

"Damn nigga I know that photography shit ain't making that much."

"Man...you know I got my little arsenal," I said not wanting to reveal everything.

"Oh yeah. Your wife." He threw up little hand quotes and laughed.

"Say what you want but she is saving our asses right now."

"Yeah, well I gotta take this money and get all this shit fixed."

"You do that and put the word out that we need some cows in here."

Cows is the term we use for high rollers. Somebody who can come in and drop a few bands but ain't on no crazy wild shooting shit.

"Imma do that but you know what I was thinking."

"What?" I asked.

"I say we have your bachelor party down here," he said. "Bring all the ballers out. We could make a half a mill easy." The shit sounded so good I couldn't pass it up.

"Let's do it. Set that shit up fam." My boy Alonzo always had the money making ideas. "And Zo... tell that nigga Tommie to give us some room. We gotta get our capital back up for this explosion."

"No doubt." We didn't necessarily owe Tommie shit. He was more of the neighborhood trap nigga that demanded we give him a cut for being on his turf.

"And tell that nigga we got robbed. Show Tommie the video."

"Show me what video?" I didn't even hear him come down the steps but there he was.

"Wassup T."

"Show me what video?" Tommie repeated. He didn't even budge when Zo said wassup.

"We got robbed last night. You heard anything about it?"

"Nope...didn't hear shit. But that doesn't affect my

money." He was like one of those fat mafia types you see on TV but instead of being white he was black.

"Yeah, it does if you can't even keep us protected in your own damn hood." I wasn't afraid of this nigga. Before I went away he wasn't shit but a penny hustler on the corner begging a motherfucker to help him out. Now, all of a sudden he was the man.

"Naw it doesn't."

"So we move shop. Go somewhere else. Stop giving you all this motherfucking money, then what?" He shrugged at that.

"Then you might get robbed again." I pulled out my pistol holding it at my side.

"And then maybe a motherfucker is going to die."

"Whoa...hold up bruh."

"Naw fuck that Zo." I was tired of pussy footing with this wannabe gangsta ass nigga.

"You know what. You got balls nigga." Tommie laughed. "Cause if I was having a bad day I would take the way you acting as disrespect."

"I'm just saying some real shit. You want us to pay you a tax and you can't control shit that happens in your own hood. What we paying you for and you ain't protecting shit?"

He nodded like he was pondering my words.

"You know what. You got a point. I'll put the word out," he said. "I guarantee ain't shit like this gonna happen again." I didn't believe him. I didn't trust shit about the snake looking motherfucker but he was here with his hand out giving me his word.

I took his hand and he stepped closer.

"But don't get it mistaken. The next time you pull a pistol out on me, I'm gonna make you use it." We locked eyes and I heard loud and clear what he was saying.

"And make no mistake," I started. "The next time you see me with a pistol it will be spitting fire. I guarantee it." Times like these I was glad I was getting out of this shit. I just needed to hit one big lick and get my money up. By the time me and Kiara get married I'm gonna be swimming in so much loot I'm not gonna be worried about no illegal poker games or no other shit. I just needed a few more weeks and all this shit would be over.

36

Dawn

As DeAndre played, Dawn traced her hands over the wedding invitations. It should have been her name there instead of Kiara's and she kept one invitation behind just so she could finish the last part of her plan.

If Orlando wasn't going to come around on his own and if Kiara wasn't going to be smart enough to connect the dots, then Dawn had one last hope.

As she cooked dinner and watched over DeAndre playing in the next room she also went to work on some research from something she saw this morning.

While holding on to Kiara's phone she saw the name Puzder come across the screen. Putting the phone to her ear, she heard his details about how badly he wanted to fuck Kiara.

That bitch acts like she is so high and mighty, Dawn thought as she typed away on her computer. She had the thought to do this weeks ago but that was before she got pregnant and saw Orlando with another woman. It was before she had to pull her pistol out and create her own diversion, shattering the windows of the club.

This idea was a lot less violent and a million times more lethal. She searched the internet and, thanks to a real estate tax website, she was able to find the most recent address to the last guest she needed to send an invitation to.

Finding a new envelope, Dawn wrote in the address for Mr. and Mrs. Puzder. *That bitch thinks she's slick but I see it all.* Dawn thought of all the early mornings when she would come over and a man would be sneaking down the steps into his Mercedes parked a few houses down.

Or the late nights when Kiara would come in smelling of men's cologne, and she knew that it definitely wasn't Orlando who she was with.

That was how she seduced Orlando in the first place. He came over to surprise Kiara, but he found Dawn instead. DeAndre was asleep and one thing lead to another as they talked and laughed. A light touch turned into a hug which lead to kissing and, before Dawn knew it, he was fucking her on the living room couch.

They finished and he left but it only took that one time to have her hooked. Dawn knew it was wrong, fucking her boss' fiance, but as time went on Dawn saw who Kiara really was. How she lied to Orlando, claiming that she had to work late but was really out with her boss.

She heard the conversations, snooped and found text messages, but now things were going too far. The wedding was close and Dawn needed to take measures into her own hands.

"What are you doing?" Spinning around Dawn was face to face with Orlando.

"I should be asking you the same thing," Dawn said. She hit a few buttons making the screen disappear as she slid the invitation carefully under the laptop.

"So you telling Ki that you pregnant by...this mystery man?" Dawn laughed as he took a few steps closer.

"You might not want to get too close," she warned. "DeAndre is in the next room."

"I don't give a fuck." He hissed. "I told you to come by the club and get the money to end this shit."

"But I don't want to…"

"You have to," Orlando insisted.

"Or what." He was close enough to kiss me and I wanted to lean in and kiss him so bad but suddenly DeAndre came running in.

"I'm hungry."

"Hey little man." Like a light switch Orlando turned on the charm and directed it to DeAndre.

"Hey O…" he gave Orlando a five like a little man.

"You ready to help me walk down this aisle?" Orlando asked him.

"You know it." As mad as I was I had to laugh at that.

"Go get cleaned up like I showed you Dre," I said. "Dinner is almost done."

"Yes ma'am." He ran off like he was a grown up going to go wash his hands but Orlando wasn't finished.

"Like I said. You have a husband. I'm about to get married."

"What if I want to be your wife?" I said.

"You can't be that. I told you that." He said it a million times. I told him that I was married but that could quickly be fixed. I never knew a man like Orlando and I didn't want to give him up. Especially not to Kiara since she was creeping her damn self. She didn't deserve him.

"But she doesn't deserve you," Dawn insisted. "She's not true to you…"

"ENOUGH. You do what the hell I said." Orlando raised his voice, his fist clenched as Dawn heard DeAndre running back towards the kitchen. Orlando backed away pretending to look in the refrigerator but the child's feeling of the bad vibes was already heightened. He walked into the kitchen cautiously looking back and forth from Dawn to Orlando trying to see what the commotion was about.

"Alright buddy go to the table. Here comes dinner." Walking straight past Orlando, Dawn tried to smile to cover up their argument but it hurt too bad. Nothing was funny, nothing was happy in life when the man you love doesn't feel the same. She wanted to hurt him, slap some sense into Orlando or anything that would force him to wake up.

He never wanted to hear the facts that Dawn had to tell him about his precious 'bride to be' Kiara. All he saw was dollar signs and to keep his cash cow he would ignore anything bad about her. Orlando made sure that Dawn couldn't get two words out about Kiara and from the beginning he made it clear that he had no intention on leaving her. But love makes people forget and after all this time Dawn prayed that maybe Orlando would change his mind.

"Alright baby here you go."

DeAndre was studying Dawn's face as she set his plate at the table. He was a deep child, like he was on the earth before but she still tried to hide her pain by smiling and trying to tickle him. DeAndre wasn't interested in the diversion. In a whisper, like he was telling me a secret, DeAndre got really close to ask a question.

"Ms. Dawn...why did Orlando yell at you? You in trouble?"

"Oh he wasn't yelling. Just grown folks talk." *Shit he heard us. Dawn scrambled to clear things up.* "We were just thinking about what to get mommy for her wedding."

"Ohhh wedding. Mommy is getting married!" he lit up

at talk about his mother walking down the aisle with the man Dawn was in love with.

"Yep, now eat up." DeAndre dived in like a grown man but back in the kitchen Orlando was fixing himself a plate. That part disgusted Dawn too, not that she didn't like to cook but it was the fact that she provided everything for him while Kiara got all of the recognition. Dawn was the one that cooked for the man, it was her food that nourished him and Dawn's pussy that fed his deepest needs.

I wanted to tell him all of that, scream it on the top of my lungs so it got through his thick skull, Dawn thought to herself but the sound of the garage opening interrupted her thoughts. That only meant the beast was home.

"MOMMY! MOMMY!" DeAndre came running through the kitchen to the garage door to welcome his mother home.

Kiara came in looking like she hadn't done anything all day. Her suit was still perfectly pressed, a briefcase in hand and a smile on her face. All the things that Dawn hated and secretly wanted for herself. She wanted to work in an office where people listened to her

"Hey baby. How are you doing?" Orlando changed from the psycho into the caring fiance in a matter of seconds. Dawn tried not to stare but it was impossible not to be in awe at the pure acting job that Orlando was doing.

"My two favorite men in the world." Orlando didn't even glance Dawn's way as he walked past her, carrying his fiancé's suitcase.

"Hey Dawn. Is dinner ready? Did you get to send those invitations out?" It was always orders with Kiara. To her, Dawn was nothing but hired help and she treated her like such.

"Yep, dinner is ready and DeAndre was eating before you walked in." The attitude in Dawn's voice was so thick it could be cut with a knife. Kiara noticed immediately and so did Orlando. He saw the future, a fight where Dawn would spill all the beans.

"Okay...great." Kiara dismissed the snark but Orlando was there to smother the fire before it started.

"Baby. Why don't you let Dawn go for the evening?" Orlando begged Kiara.

"We need to start handling things like a family." No woman could argue with that plea from her man.

"Oh..yeah that's fine. Go enjoy your night Dawn. You're dismissed. See you in the morning." Dawn gathered her things as Kiara flicked her wrist and banished her away.

"Bye Ms. Dawn." DeAndre was the only one who showed me any kind of affection.

"Bye DeAndre. See you tomorrow." Dawn carried her things out as she heard the trio laughing and joking while they piled food on their plates that Dawn slaved over all afternoon.

I'm going to show you bitch, she silently promised her employer as she left the house. Getting to her car Dawn set out to find the first mailbox she could. There was one final invitation that needed to go out, an unexpected guest that needed to be in attendance for the union of Kiara and Orlando. It was Dawn's job to make sure that they get there.

37

Kiara
KIARA

There was nothing better than getting home and being greeted by my man and my son. Now that we ate, talked, and gave DeAndre his bath, it was time for me to have my nightly ritual with my son.

"Okay son. Pick out a book." It was reading time, and since Orlando was on a business call I did this part alone but pretty soon we would be putting DeAndre to bed together.

"Mommy, I don't want to read a book."

"Why not?" DeAndre looked around like there was someone going to jump out at him.

"You can tell me son," I said. He never acted like this, but tonight he seemed a little sad. I figured maybe he was tired but now my antennas were up.

"Mr. Orlando yelled at Ms. Dawn."

"He did...why?" DeAndre shrugged. "And she was crying. I want to hug her Mommy." Now I was confused. What the hell could Orlando have been yelling at her about?

"I know, but it's nothing baby. It's going to be okay." I

gave him a hug and he squeezed me back like he was afraid for his life.

"Mommy, is he going to yell at me?" That was a good question. I tried to integrate Orlando into our lives as much as possible but with him working and my no overnights rule it was getting hard for us to come together as a family.

"No honey. Of course not," I tried to reassure him as my mind was moving now in a million different places. What if Orlando and DeAndre didn't get along? I didn't think it was possible for a three-year-old and an adult to have issues but now I was seeing for myself that something was off.

I read DeAndre his story like always and he fell asleep before I reached the end. But before I tiptoed out of his room I already had a plan.

A good attorney always thinks of a strategy for approaching questioning and I already had mine down pat before I met up with Orlando in the living room.

"You done with your call boo?"

"Yep, just got off,"

"Whoo...man I had a long day." Sitting down beside him I told him about my day or at least the parts I was willing to share. I left out that I had a meeting with HR about Puzder... but everything else I told him.

"Yeah, I had a few issues today but I got them smoothed out. But hey boo I wanna talk to you. I think you should hire a new nanny," he said. I said nothing just listening but the words that seeped out of his mouth was a perfect setup for my questioning.

"Really? Why?"

"I think when we get married we should start over with a new nanny and a new place so we can grow as a family."

"Wow, thats a good idea but DeAndre likes Dawn. You think she's not good?"

"I mean. She has a bit of an attitude problem and frankly, I think she's jealous of you." I had to laugh at that. Who wasn't jealous of me was a better statement to make but I said nothing.

"Maybe boo. I'll think on it. You let me know if she doesn't something you don't approve of."

"Oh I can make a list on this shit she doesn't do." *Whenever a man started you better pay attention.* DeWayne used to tell me that all the time and right now my ears were wide open.

"Well you let me know then baby. Because I can't have no foolishness around us," I said, laughing. "But I think I'm about to go to sleep."

"Damn...you sure you don't want me to spend the night? DeAndre will never know." He smiled, pulling me close. Any other time I would have welcomed a companion but right now I had too much to think about.

"Nope, we're gonna stick to it," I said. "Just for a couple more weeks."

"Aww damn. Alright."

"And where is the other car?" I asked. "Why you driving the truck?"

"Oh I got two flats at the same time today. Had to get some new tires."

"Damn baby. That's messed up." I walked him to the door holding hands like nothing was wrong. But inside all alarms were going off. Nothing seemed right and for all of a sudden Orlando to start wanting Dawn gone only meant one thing. The bitch must really want what I have. I saw the way she looked at me tonight, rolling her eyes as I came through the door. I only tried to help her and now she was probably getting jealous because she was pregnant by this mystery dude and her husband was overseas. But tonight I was about to fix all of that.

"In a few weeks I will be here to stay."

"I can't wait." Giving my man a kiss and a wave as I watched him get into his car and disappear.

But I wasn't going to sleep.

I had work to do and luckily for Dawn I already knew who to contact. Getting my phone and slipping into my office, I made a call.

"Hello." His voice was raspy and old but still at nine o'clock at night he answered the phone for me.

"Judge McCaskill. Sorry to disturb you. This is Kiara Lawrence."

"I know who it is Lawrence. It says it on my phone." He laughed. "What the hell do you want at this hour."

"Well sir, I was hoping you could help me. You see a friend of mine has a husband who is deployed and she is facing some medical issues with her pregnancy and desperately needs the husband to come back home."

"Oh...what is his name?"

"Sergeant Paul Powell." I gave the judge Paul's full credentials, letting him know everything I did.

"And how badly do you need this done?"

"Desperately sir," I said. "Or I wouldn't have notified you."

"I guess we will consider this a favor fulfilling the job you did for my son in law last year."

"Yes sir. How is Jimmy anyway? Is he staying out of trouble?" I cleared his son on a vehicular manslaughter charge the previous year. Doing such a good job that Jimmy was found not guilty and was free to go. That and a few strings I pulled gained me a favor in the judge's eyes, now I needed that gift to be repaid.

"Certainly sir. That sounds fair." Clearing his throat I could tell he was thinking.

"Fine. I'll call my contacts in the morning. Get this done."

"Thanks sir." He didn't say a word more and then the phone just went dead. That was the judge's style. He didn't do shit nicely, he was a bear to deal with but a bear that would get this done. Dawn's husband would be back in the states and she would stop with this jealousy bullshit.

Before I could put my phone down, again it rang and Puzder's name appeared on the screen.

"Hello," I said.

"You bitch." I pressed the button to record immediately.

"I'm sorry sir what did you say."

"I said you raggedy bitch. You reported me to HR for sexual harassment." I didn't say a word.

"Hello."

"Yes I'm here."

"So you aren't going to answer my question," he said.

"Sir, I don't know why you are harassing me." I sounded so innocent and it only pissed Puzder off more. He sounded mad enough to come through the phone but I continued to play coy in a way that only I could while at the same time keeping him talking.

"I wasn't harassing you when you were sucking my dick and I gave you a promotion."

"Sir you made me do that," I said. "You told me I had to…"

"God dammit quit fucking saying that. You wanted it. Just admit it. You wanted it." He was yelling at the top of his lungs now. I had enough ammunition on Puzder that I would probably get a seven figure settlement out of this.

"Mr. Puzder I have to go."

"No...No don't you hang up you cunt..." But I did anyway. Pressing end and saving the recorded conversation to hand over to HR in the morning. In no time Puzder would be gone and I would take his place.

It was like the stars were aligning and after losing so much it finally felt like I was getting what I wanted. But I kept having this feeling like the ground was going to fall out from under me at any minute... but I knew that was impossible. I had dotted my i's and crossed my t's. Nothing was going to stop me now...not one damn thing.

38

Ariane

In the middle of the dark he was behind me with a hand full of my hair in his fist. I loved this shit, and at the top of my lungs I let Orlando know how much I loved it.

"Fuck me...Fuck me...Please fuck me," I begged him over and over as Orlando pushed deeper and deeper inside me. It felt good to be fucked by a boss, but even better to be fucking that bitch Kiara's man. We spent almost every night together the past few weeks but now it was crunch time. He told me that he was marrying that bitch in a few days and now with every muscle in my pussy I was trying hard to stop him from marrying that raggedy bitch.

"Shit girl. You putting it on a nigga." I was trying squeezing my pussy like a vice grip on his dick praying with every stroke he would change his mind.

"Shit I'm cumming." I made sure not to move making sure he couldn't pull out of me fast enough and over the last week or so he wasn't trying to.

"Damn girl," he was out of breath, finally falling out of me.

"Yeah now you sure you wanna get married?"

Through the dark I could see his expression change. I had spoken too soon. I tried to be quiet and just make subtle suggestions but good dick will make you forget all of your thoughts.

"What I tell you when we first got together?" Orlando shuffled around a little bit and a few seconds later the lights came on. He was already standing up, pulling his pants on.

"Wait...where are you going?"

"I'm leaving man. I come over here to chill and you always on some bullshit."

"Always...we only been fucking around for a few weeks."

"And when we started I told you that I was getting married and you gonna be my side bitch. You agreed to that." I did agree, but he didn't know what my motivation was. He had no idea why I'm doing this.

"Baby can you be mad that I want you all to myself?" He kept getting ready, pulling on his shirt quicker than I could talk. "Baby do you hear me?"

"Naw I don't hear shit," he said. "I thought yo ass was different." Before he made it to the door I was on my feet.

"No...wait."

"Wait for what? I'm not fucking playing if you can't play your position then don't fucking play with me."

"I can...I can do it," I insisted.

"Then prove it." He had been asking me little shit for weeks. Would I do anything for him, was I ride or die material, what did I go to jail for, and would I go back if I had to. All shit that I said yes to because it was true. I was willing to do whatever to get him away from that bitch... he just had no idea why I would do anything for him.

"How do you want me to prove it?" I asked.

"I want you to work a game for me tomorrow night."

He had been explaining over and over about some poker games he did but the shit didn't make sense to me.

"So what you want me to do?"

"Tomorrow, I want you to just waitress at the spot," Orlando explained. "Bring people more chips and cash them out."

"Then what."

"You do that for me I'll know you're down."

"Cool. I can do that." He kissed me as I tried pulling his shirt off and getting him in the bed but that didn't work.

His phone rang and I already knew it had to be that bitch. He answered it and I did what I always did, sat on the bed, quiet like a mouse.

"Yeah...I told you I paid the caterer already." My mind jumped when I heard that. "Alrighty baby. Talk to you later." No sooner than he hung up the phone did I start back with the questions.

"What was that about...a caterer."

"I told you man...I'm still going through with it," Orlando said. "I'm getting this bread so either you gonna be fucking with me or what."

"I'm with you. I'm just saying you talking like you getting married tomorrow." He didn't say shit. "So when are you?"

"That's my business. Just have yo ass ready to go tomorrow night." He pulled his keys out of his pocket and that let me know the night was over.

"Okay...I'll be ready."

"Cool...I'll call you." With a kiss on my forehead he left me naked in the middle of my bed with his cum seeping out my pussy. I told him that I was on birth control, he even gave me money to pay for it saying he liked to be all natural with his women. Little did he know I've been off birth control for weeks.

In my nightstand there were fertility pills, top of the line that were sure to get me pregnant. For now I would play this game with him... but before long I was going to be pregnant with his child and then he would have to explain to his 'wifey to be' how he got me pregnant.

I kept imagining the look on her face when she sees me with a big belly. That look and her heart breaking was the shit that kept me alive. I said after being with DeWayne that I wasn't going to play this side chick shit anymore but to get back at Kiara I was willing to do anything. Even by getting pregnant by a big dick that I barely knew.

39

Kiara
KIARA

I should have been off. It was the day before my wedding, but I was still at work wrapping up some loose ends when I was asked to come down to HR. Now, instead of being in my office working, I was in front of the HR legal team, my lawyer, Puzder and his lawyer. I knew this was going to be interesting.

"Thank you everyone for coming down under such short notice. We wanted to get things handled before Ms. Lawrence goes on vacation," the HR manager started off but Puzder always has to be the center of attention.

"Yeah, she's going on leave so she can fuck somebody else's life up." Puzder had been on leave for a week or so now and it showed. The man sitting on the other side of the table looked disheveled with an unshaved face and wrinkled tracksuit. With every word he spoke a pungent smell of alcohol filled the room. His lawyer whispered something into his ear as the rest of the people in the room gave him a cold glare.

"Well, we wanted to express extreme regret to Ms. Lawrence, and Mr. Puzder is here to apologize as well."

"Apologize," he scoffed. "I ain't apologizing for shit. This bitch ruined my life with those recordings."

"Sir...calm down," security asked but that only made things worse. Meanwhile I tried sitting with a straight face to keep from laughing.

"No no, she played the game and now y'all wanna give her money and an apology." That's exactly what they were doing. I would be on paid leave for two months to "recuperate from the mental stress." And then I would be coming back to a promotion, pay raise, and a nice package to basically keep me quiet.

"No, fuck...that...I..." Puzder tried to get up but he began to shake.

"Sir, are you okay?" He didn't answer, his arms grabbing for the table as he fell out of his chair.

"Someone call 911. He's having a heart attack." I was frozen in time looking around the room as people scrambled to help him.

"Come on...let's leave," my lawyer pulled me outside as people ran in scrambling. In the hall, my lawyer Anthony Turner, didn't seem fazed.

"That bastard got what he deserved," Anthony whispered as he slid the manilla envelope containing my offer into my hands. "Congrats, you are officially a millionaire." He laughed but I kept fighting the urge to go back into that room and make sure Puzder was okay. I didn't hate the man, this was just business.

"OUT OF THE WAY PLEASE." The EMT'ss came in quickly, going into the room and bringing Puzder out on a stretcher. He looked at me as they brought him out, at least his eyes were trained on me. It sent a chill through my body and for the first time in a long time I felt like shit.

"Congrats," Anthony continued. "Go home and get

some rest. It's your big day tomorrow! " I broke out of my trance to see Anthony's smiling face.

"Umm yeah," I said, hazily. "Tomorrow it is."

"Well, you got a lot to do. Get out of here." He acted like nothing happened. Like a man didn't just have a heart attack in front of us. I guess I'm turning into one of them because, like Anthony said, I told the HR people good bye signing my contract and I left the building to start my vacation but I couldn't shake Puzder's eyes. His glare made me feel dirty all over and for the first time I questioned my whole life.

Lord let him be okay, I prayed as I walked to the car. If he wasn't, then the blood would be on my hands.

40

Dawn

Dear Ms, Powell,
 Thank you for your dedication but effective immediately I will no longer need your services....

Dawn read over the letter in disbelief. The last time she saw Kiara she was giving her the week off and now today in the mail Dawn receives a certified letter with a forced resignation.

She was already having a bad day but this made it worse. She had morning sickness so intense that she couldn't get dressed without vomiting. Pregnancy books were all over her room with a trashcan planted by her bed just in case she couldn't make it to the bathroom.

Now, as she was trying to get her energy up she gets a knock at the door with this letter.

"This is bullshit." She said aloud to the room.

She had been dodging Orlando trying to figure out what she was going to do when out of nowhere Kiara released her of her services for a week. Now the letter with no explanation of why she was being terminated.

She dialed Kiara's number readying herself to ask for an explanation when she heard her front door slam.

Dawn thought she had to be hearing things.

"Hello?" Dawn yelled out as she looked for something to protect herself but there was nothing at her disposal but a thick pregnancy book.

"Baby it's me...I'm home." She hadn't heard his voice in so long but the closer the steps got the more she drifted into a panic.

"Paul..."

"Yeah baby it's me." He was in her bedroom in full uniform but she still didn't believe he was real.

"Oh my God!" Dawn jumped into his arms and they squeezed each other tight. "What are you doing here?"

"Baby I had to come make sure you're okay...I came back to..." he stopped mid sentence and eased her back down to the floor as he looked over the bed. Every pregnancy book in God's creation was scattered across the sheets.

"What's this?"

"Umm..." Dawn could tell he was already putting two and two together. Looking from the bed back to her and she had no words to explain what was going on. .

"Are you?" Dawn didn't know what to say. Her stomach had already begun poking out and the evidence was all over the bed.

"Oh shit...that's why she pulled the strings..." Paul said.

"Who?"

"Wait a minute." He began rubbing his head.

"How far along are you?" he wanted to know. "I haven't been home in a year..." Dawn wanted to lie but there was nothing she could say. She was stuck with the truth.

"You cheated on me!" It was more of an accusation than a question.

"Baby…" She reached out to touch him but he pushed her away. Paul still had on his uniform looking handsome but the devastation on his face was like someone died.

"I knew it." Paul said shaking his head, his hand balling into a fist of rage.

"Baby it just happened. It's a long story…" Before she could say another word Paul grabbed a small glass from the nightstand and threw it down to the floor.

Damn jumped on the bed in fear of the glass and of the man in front of her. He didn't step toward her, instead he glared at her almost growling his words like an angry junk yard dog.

"And it's your boss that was trying to get me home to help you. I bet you didn't tell her it's not my baby."

"What?"

"You heard me. People try to help you and you always fucking shit up. I want yo ass out of here by the end of the week." Paul stomped out of the house slamming the door but what he said left Dawn's ears ringing.

What did he mean my boss got him back here. She thought about it and it all made sense. Why would Kiara give her the week off and why had she been so nice lately asking her more and more about Paul?

"That bitch…she knows." Dawn scrambled to her feet, avoiding the broken glass trying to get to her phone.

She had to tell Orlando. His phone rang a bunch of times before she heard loud music come on the line.

"HELLO!"

"SHE KNOWS!" Dawn screamed.

"WHAT! I CAN'T HEAR YOU." The tears were falling down her face, her hand over her belly as she tried to figure out what this meant for her and the unborn baby.

"I SAID SHE KNOWS…"

"KNOWS WHAT?" Dawn tried to tell him, battling with the loud music and her failing voice mixed with angry tears. But Orlando had no time for her to get the words out.

"I'LL CALL YOU LATER!" Orlando promptly hung up leaving Dawn staring at the phone in disbelief.

"ORLANDO…ORLANDO?" Dawn screamed but he wasn't there. "Oh no…no no no no…" She tried calling again, hitting redial over and over but there was no answer.

She was now pregnant, unemployed, soon to be homeless and probably divorced.

"You bitch. You're going to pay for this." She screamed through the house. "You wanna play bitch." She went to her dresser, pulling out a gun from her drawer and counting the bullets. "We can play alright bitch."

41

Orlando

The room was crowded and there was money all over the place. With all of this going on I don't even know why I answered the phone for that bum ass bitch Dawn, but all I wanted to know from her was when did she plan on getting this abortion. I didn't know what that bitch was saying and if it wasn't that I wanted her to lose my number.

Kiara already agreed to fire her ass but I needed that baby to be gone too. But that shit would have to wait for another day. Right now all I knew was the poker game was packed and all I saw was money all over the place. Downstairs in the basement of the store we had this bitch popping like a full blown casino. Music bumping with the drinks, food, and especially money flowing. I couldn't have asked for anything better and to think a few weeks ago I was afraid of losing a punk ass 140k. Today I knew we were up by almost 200k and the night wasn't even over yet.

"Congratulations nigga." People were screaming all around the room but I wasn't sure if they were happy about me getting married or the party but all I could see was Ariane's ass working the floor.

She was getting drinks, cashing people out, and she did it all with a smile.

"You my rider ain't you," I whispered in her ear when she finally had a second to sit down.

"I told you I was." She smiled over the music but she was a predictable ass bitch. It was always a gullible hoe like her around and I was going to make money off this hoe.

"I just need you to keep cashing out and…" I couldn't finish my thought before I heard screaming and the sound of an explosion.

"FREEZE POLICE!" People tried scrambling, money flew up in the air and before I could move I saw a gun in my face.

"GET YOUR ASS DOWN ON THE GROUND." I did as they said, not moving and not wanting to be shot. Pulling me up to my foot one of the officers pinned me against the wall.

"Who the fuck is in charge of this." I didn't hesitate, Ariane was a few feet away tears already running down her face.

"Ahh man. It's her and this other nigga around here named Tommie. I'm getting married tomorrow and I'm just trying to enjoy myself." You always had to be set for shit like this. The attendees always got away but whoever was planning the party was the one the cops were looking for.

"HER…HER RIGHT THERE." Ariane was already crying but she was too busy with a cop in her face to say a word.

"Yeah she got the money on her. Look at her. She got the keys." I kept it that way, giving the little bitch I'm fucking with at any given time the keys. If Dawn would have shut her fucking mouth and did as I told her she would be here. Most people were being let go and as I looked the cop in his eyes he turned me around and took the handcuffs off.

"You're free to go." The color drained from Ariane's face but I didn't look at her too long. I trained her these last few weeks to be a down bitch. I told her to play her role, as I left I gave her a wink. Just a signal to tell her to keep her mouth shut and giving her the thought that I would fix this but I wasn't fucking with her. She got in this shit on her own, now she had to get out.

42

Kiara

The look of Puzder having a heart attack haunted me all night and all through the day. As I got dressed slipping on my wedding gown with my family around and all my bridesmaids, I kept seeing his face. Those piercing eyes made my heart break; yeah I wanted his ass to suffer but I didn't want him to have a heart attack.

And now because of the agreement I had no way to figure out what happened to him.

"You okay Ki…" My sister and maid of honor asked.

"Yeah I'm good," I said. "Just ready to get this going."

"Well, it's time."

"Do they have DeAndre, what about the flutist, and are the caterers in place, and the…"

"Girl…calm down." I looked into Keira's eyes. I wanted to tell her so bad about the things I did and what I had been through. "I just…I need to talk to someone."

"It's time ladies," someone said from behind us. There was no time to do anything, we had to go.

I didn't know how to figure out what happened to Puzder and right now I had no time.

"Lineup. Here the bride goes here." There were people everywhere and everyone telling me how beautiful I looked. I did look nice but, too bad, I didn't feel it. Giving a final glance over myself as looked in the mirror I didn't even recognize the person staring back at me.

Time had taken its toll... I was beautiful on the outside but inside? Man, I didn't know who I was.

The music started and before I knew it I was watching people walk in. I saw Orlando and DeAndre was up ahead carrying in the rings.

Mommy is he going to yell at me. I heard his little voice breaking through the music and as I blinked ahead I saw a mirage of DeWayne. It was as if he was giving me a signal from the grave. It could have been his ghost or just my imagination but he didn't look happy, he was shaking his head as if to tell me something wasn't right.

"Ki...it's your turn baby." I snapped back and noticed the music changed. It was my turn now to walk down the aisle, seeing everyone smiling and snapping pictures. Looking to the front seeing the smile on Orlando's face was great but it wasn't what I imagined. This wasn't the explosive moment that I dreamed of, but I kept moving.

"WAIT...STOP!!!" Someone screamed from behind me. "WAIT IT'S FAKE. ALL OF THIS SHIT. HE DOESN'T LOVE HER." Turning around I locked eyes with Dawn.

"Look...this is his baby." The music stopped just as pictures flew up in the air like confetti and when they fell cascading over the entire church I made out the black and white ultrasound photo.

"THIS IS HIS BABY!"

"Dawn...get the hell out of here." Orlando yelled.

I looked back and forth from Orlando to her and the anger that went across his face let me know it was true.

"So... you are the mystery guy?" He was at my side with no words as people began grabbing the papers like money falling from the sky.

"DAWN...LEAVE!" Orlando screamed as he tried pulling me to the alter.

"NO! My baby won't be silenced for you and that bitch." The church gasped. I turned to my son, the pillow he was holding with our marital rings was drooping as DeAndre began to cry.

"Kiera. Get my son out of here." Turning back around I saw someone standing next to Dawn. I couldn't believe it, I hadn't seen her in years.

"Attorney Lawrence." Her voice was loud and pierced all the commotion and even Dawn's screaming. "You've been fucking my husband you dirty bitch." Everyone in the church gasped. It was like a damn soap opera and everyone was getting exposed. "Then you send us an invitation to your wedding." She held up one of my invitations but I never sent her anything. My words were caught in my throat as I saw a smile spread across Dawn's face.

"THIS BITCH FUCKED MY HUSBAND AND GOT HIM FIRED FROM A FIRM HE HELPED BUILD." Mrs. Puzder shouted letting the words echo through the church.

"AND YOU KILLED MY HUSBAND!" Killed? Was Puzder dead? Before I could say a word I saw the gun down at her side. She looked crazed with her hair every which way and her clothes weren't the familiar business attire but a college t-shirt and sweat pants. "And now I'm going to kill yours." I heard the words but didn't believe it. I couldn't move or breath I was stuck to the floor. It was fate all over again coming to take someone that I loved.

43

Orlando

The gun went up and all I saw was Dawn sprinting towards me. Through the crowd she made it, twisting around just as I saw the pistol go up.

"NOOO!!!" But it was too late. The gun went off and I saw Dawn's smile turn into pain.

"NOO…"

"She's pregnant with my baby." I heard the yelp come from Kiara's mouth but she didn't need to be surprised anymore. After the shit I saw today she has been up to way more than I thought. I knew she was fucking somebody at work but what had she done to take it this far?!

"Call the ambulance. CALL 911." Blood didn't seem that bad and Dawn was back smiling.

"See, I told you I would die for you." I held her in my arms, it looked like the bullet went straight through her arm but I wasn't sure.

"Yep you did. Stay with me. You and the baby stay with me." It was like no one else existed but her and my white tux was now covered in her blood, but I didn't care.

The lady with the gun was now on the floor being held

down by a dozen people, but Kiara was up now standing over us. Her eyes were on my face burning a hole through me.

"I'm here. Just concentrate on me."

"I love you so much." Dawn said with tears falling from her eyes.

"Orlando." Kiara called to me but I didn't even bother to look up. It was over, it was never going to work anyway. I just wanted the money. I needed to feel like I was worth something and money was the only way for me to feel that power.

Now, none of that mattered. I heard the sirens getting closer and closer praying that they made it in time to save Dawn and my baby.

"Paramedics. Get back." Everyone moved, Kiara was long gone but I was still there walking with Dawn as they wheeled her away.

"Will she be okay? She's pregnant." I asked about a dozen times on our way to the ambulance.

"We'll do the best we can sir. But it looks like it went straight through."

That was good news. Getting into the back of the ambulance I was asking the Lord for help. This was my wake up call but Dawn was only trying to save me.

They didn't deserve this, this was my fault and these were my sins coming back to haunt me. I just didn't want my seed to die for it.

44

Kiara

My wedding dress was gone and the makeup was all cried and smeared off... the only thing that remained from the wedding was my updo. I was now in sweat pants walking through the hospital to the waiting room. I had to talk to him face to face but when I saw him in the waiting room I felt nothing.

His white tux was smeared with blood and now staring at him as I walked into the waiting area this seemed like a dream. We were supposed to be on a plane right now headed to our honeymoon. Maybe none of that was meant to be.

"Orlando." His head popped up but when he realized it was me and a look of shame mixed with panic crossed his face.

"Is she alive?" I asked.

"Do you really care?" I did care, I didn't feel like anyone else needed to die no matter how mad I was.

"Just answer the question."

"Yes, she's alive and so is the baby. She's resting but she

doesn't want to see you." Orlando told me as if it were going to hurt my feelings.

"I'm not interested in seeing her. But thanks. I'm here to talk to you."

"C'mon with the bullshit, K. You didn't really love me." He was right but I had something to say about him as well.

"You didn't love me either," I said. "I know you've been fucking bitches behind my back... but the nanny, really?" He looked down, probably ashamed but it was too late for that. "Yeah I can't understand why you would make it that close to home. But whatever."

"You fucked your boss," Orlando came back at me.

"Yeah I did. And I'm going to have to pay for that." I shook my head trying to rid myself of the thoughts.

"But I just wanted to come up here in person and tell you it's through. Truthfully, it never really was real to begin with."

He was right about that, it wasn't.

"I see why that other bitch wanted to get back at you."

"What?" Now I didn't understand.

"Nothing." He brushed the statement off and inside I already knew who he was talking about.

"Well I guess this is goodbye." He said standing up like he wanted to give me a hug but I backed away.

"No, this is good riddance." I had already married one fucked up man in my life and with him I was about to marry a second. We stared at each other until a voice broke our glares at each other.

"You'll never find somebody like me. Never…and to think I was gonna marry your clown ass." I stared at him for a moment, seeing the layer of monster skin fall off him.

"Yeah you're right…and I don't want to find someone

else like you." I was about to lite into his ass but we were interrupted.

"The Powell Family." He looked up as a nurse came over. She looked from him to me but I pointed in his direction as I walked away leaving both of them in my past. It was time for me to go into my future but going back through the hospital to my car there was one person on my mind now.

Taking out my phone I made a few calls on the way back to my car. It was time that I reconcile everything from my past. To move forward I didn't want any bad karma on me or my son and to fix that I had to be the bigger woman... for once in my life.

Months Later

45

Kiara

I figured out my problem, I left too many loose ends. From Puzder, God rest his soul, all the way down to Ariane. I had left too much open and available for someone to hurt me.

Dawn hurt me badly but that was my fault, leaving my man around another woman. And in the first place I should have never been involved with Orlando. I went on that vacation, but instead I went with my son. I had to figure out how I kept putting myself in these bad places, and for that I needed a little help.

Just a few dollars, a private detective, and poof... I had the entire lay of the land. I saw where I messed up with Orlando and I uncovered who he really was and the more I looked into it the worse things got. How I ever thought about marrying him was beyond me, but one thing was for sure. He wasn't going to get off that easy.

He took my money and embarrassed me in front of people. Damn the shooting but that bitch showing up with ultrasound pictures that she threw in the air like confetti was enough for me.

Now in the courthouse I was here to make a connection with someone that had just as much interest as I did in seeing Orlando go down.

Walking through the court halls I found room 459 and walked to the front waiting for my case to be called. Since quitting my position at the firm, I now had time to do something for the people, and serve my own interests.

"Ariane Collins vs The State. Will representation for the defendant please come forth?" That was my cue, and walking across the bar I took my place on the defendant's side waiting on my client. Whether she knew it or not, Ariane and I weren't finished. We had just begun.

46

Ariane
ARIANE

Three months in county was probably harder than all of my months in the FEDs. Now walking to court with shackles on my feet I was expecting to finally tell my side to the judge. He probably wouldn't care but I was going to tell it anyway.

The courtroom was filled and all I could think about was this court appointed lawyer they were going to give me. But as I walked into the bright lights of the court I thought I was seeing things. It had to be a mirage, because no way was Kiara standing were my lawyer should have been.

"What are you doing here?" I whispered to her.

"About to save your ass." The bailiff allowed us to sit but Kiara stayed standing.

"Your honor I present to you exhibit A. A record of all of the infractions at the Porter Convenience store where the infraction took place. These incidents go back almost ten years. The defendant could not have been a contributor to this enterprise as she was incarcerated at the inception of this enterprise. She was simply working to pay child support for her young daughter." Kiara may have been a bitch but she was a bad bitch in this courtroom.

"In exchange for her immediate release and charges being dropped Ms. Collins will supply all of the knowledge that she possesses about this enterprise." All I heard was snitching. I fumbled around in the chair trying to get Kiara's attention because there was no way I would be a snitch.

"What?" She hissed at me as the prosecutor spoke.

"I don't want to be a snitch."

"Excuse me your honor let me have a word with my client."

"Make it brief." She smiled briefly at the judge as she bent down to speak with me.

"Look. Either you tell or your going back to jail and it's ten years this time. And you won't see your daughter. You were trying to get back at me. I get it. But that shits over so you give up Orlando or you go to jail."

"But he's your husband." A smirk crossed her face. "He was supposed to be…but that didn't happen." That was all I needed to hear. Because of him I probably had to start all the way over now after spending three months in this shit hole. But three months was better than ten years.

"So what do you say? Let's burn his ass." She put out her hand to shake mine. "Side bitches unite," I looked at her hand then back at her smiling face. I couldn't do anything but smile right back. "Side Bitches unite," we said as we both smiled at each other. I was done being enemies, it was always the men that got in our way. Now it's time we make these motherfuckers pay for what they've done to us because nothing is sweeter than revenge.

Thank You for Reading

<u>More Titles By Solae</u>
Sex and Shade
Side Chick Scorned
What's Done in the Dark Series
Seduced By a Thug
Down Low Cartel
Hubby Vs Bae
Tales of a Real Freak
Cuffing Season
Down Low Thuggin
AdDICKted
Shades of the Projects
And Many more…
Visit SolaeDehvine.com to get all of Solae's stories

TEXT SOLAE
To
313131

*For New Releases
and
Free Book Promos*